BASED ON THE ORIGINAL CHARACTERS CREATED BY

JIM DAViS

GRAPHIC NOVELS AVAILABLE FROM PAPERCUTZ ™

GRAPHIC NOVEL #1
"FISH TO FRY"

GRAPHIC NOVEL #2
"THE CURSE OF
THE CAT PEOPLE"

GRAPHIC NOVEL #3
"CATZILLA"

GRAPHIC NOVEL #4
"CAROLING CAPERS"

GRAPHIC NOVEL #5
"A GAME OF CAT
AND MOUSE"

COMING SOON:

GRAPHIC NOVEL #6
"MOTHER GARFIELD"

GARFIELD & Co 5 - A GAME OF CAT AND MOUSE
"THE GARFIELD SHOW" SERIES © 2012- DARGAUD MEDIA.
ALL RIGHTS RESERVED. © PAWS. "GARFIELD" & GARFIELD
CHARACTERS ™ & © PAWS INC.- ALL RIGHTS RESERVED.
THE GARFIELD SHOW- A DARGAUD MEDIA PRODUCTION.
IN ASSOCIATION WITH FRANCE3 WITH THE PARTICIPATION
OF CENTRE NATIONAL DE LA CINÉMETOGRAPHIE AND THE
SUPPORT OF REGION ILE-DE-FRANCE. A SERIES DEVELOPED
BY PHILIPPE VIDAL, ROBERT REA & STEVE BALISSAT. BASED
UPON THE CHARACTERS CREATED BY JIM DAVIS.
ORIGINAL STORIES BY MATHILDE MARANINCHI & ANTONIN
POIRÉE (CATNAP), MIKE PULEY (PETMATCHERS), AND
CHRISTOPHE POUJOL (A GAME OF CAT AND MOUSE).

CEDRIC MICHIELS - COMICS ADAPTATION
JOE JOHNSON - TRANSLATIONS
JANICE CHIANG - LETTERING
MICHAEL PETRANEK - PRODUCTION
MICHAEL PETRANEK - ASSOCIATE EDITOR
JIM SALICRUP
EDITOR-IN-CHIEF

ISBN: 978-1-59707-300-4

PRINTED IN CHINA
FEBRUARY 2012 BY O.G. PRINTING PRODUCTIONS, LTD.
UNITS 2 & 3, 5/F, LEMMI CENTRE
50 HOI YUEN ROAD
KWON TONG, KOWLOON

DISTRIBUTED BY MACMILLAN
FIRST PAPERCUTZ PRINTING

GARFIELD & Co GRAPHIC NOVELS ARE AVAILABLE AT BOOK-
SELLERS EVERYWHERE IN HARDCOVER ONLY FOR $7.99 EACH.

OR ORDER FROM US - PLEASE ADD $4.00 FOR POSTAGE AND HANDLING FOR
THE FIRST BOOK, ADD $1.00 FOR EACH ADDITIONAL BOOK. PLEASE MAKE CHECK
PAYABLE TO: NBM PUBLISHING SEND TO: PAPERCUTZ, 40 EXCHANGE PLACE,
STE. 1308, NEW YORK, NY 10005 (1-800-886-1223)

WWW.PAPERCUTZ.COM

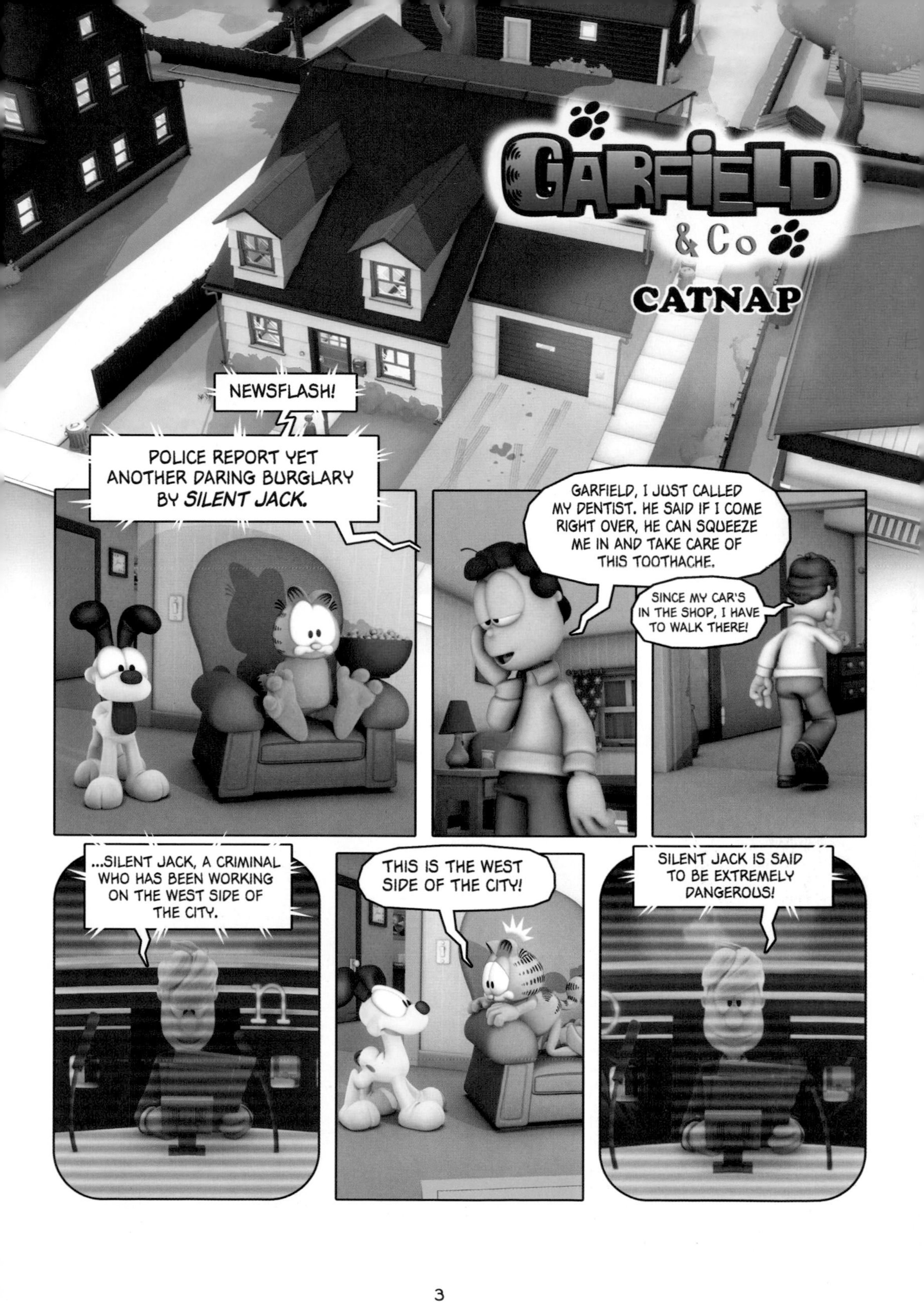
GARFIELD & Co
CATNAP
NEWSFLASH!
POLICE REPORT YET ANOTHER DARING BURGLARY BY SILENT JACK.
GARFIELD, I JUST CALLED MY DENTIST. HE SAID IF I COME RIGHT OVER, HE CAN SQUEEZE ME IN AND TAKE CARE OF THIS TOOTHACHE.
SINCE MY CAR'S IN THE SHOP, I HAVE TO WALK THERE!
...SILENT JACK, A CRIMINAL WHO HAS BEEN WORKING ON THE WEST SIDE OF THE CITY.
THIS IS THE WEST SIDE OF THE CITY!
SILENT JACK IS SAID TO BE EXTREMELY DANGEROUS!

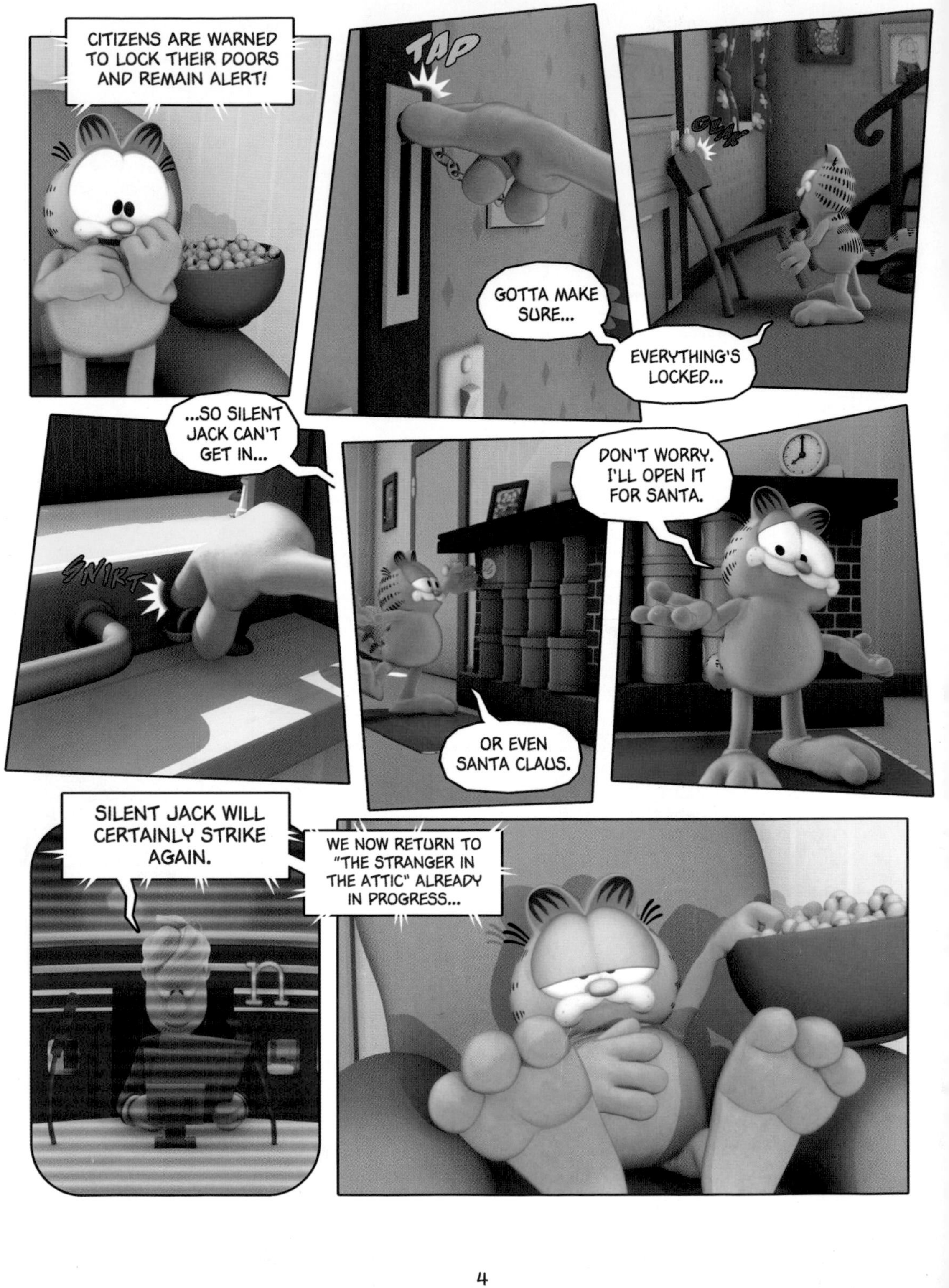
CITIZENS ARE WARNED TO LOCK THEIR DOORS AND REMAIN ALERT!
TAP
GOTTA MAKE SURE...
EVERYTHING'S LOCKED...
...SO SILENT JACK CAN'T GET IN...
SNIKT
OR EVEN SANTA CLAUS.
DON'T WORRY. I'LL OPEN IT FOR SANTA.
SILENT JACK WILL CERTAINLY STRIKE AGAIN.
WE NOW RETURN TO "THE STRANGER IN THE ATTIC" ALREADY IN PROGRESS...

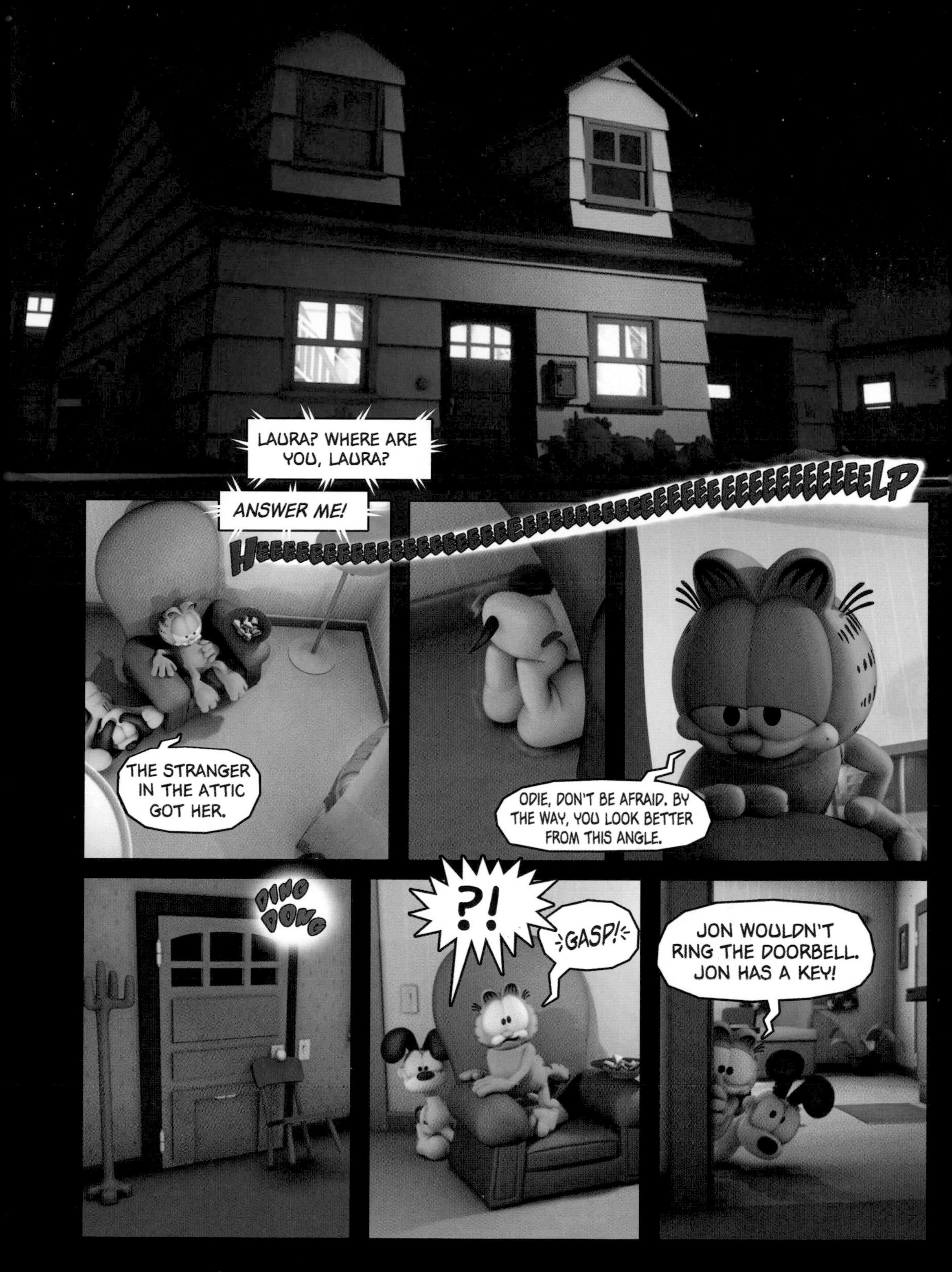

LAURA? WHERE ARE YOU, LAURA?
ANSWER ME!
HEEEEEEEEEEEEEEEEEEEEEEEEEEEEEEEEEEEEEEEEEEEEEEEEEEEEELP
THE STRANGER IN THE ATTIC GOT HER.
ODIE, DON'T BE AFRAID. BY THE WAY, YOU LOOK BETTER FROM THIS ANGLE.
DING DONG
?!
GASP!
JON WOULDN'T RING THE DOORBELL. JON HAS A KEY!

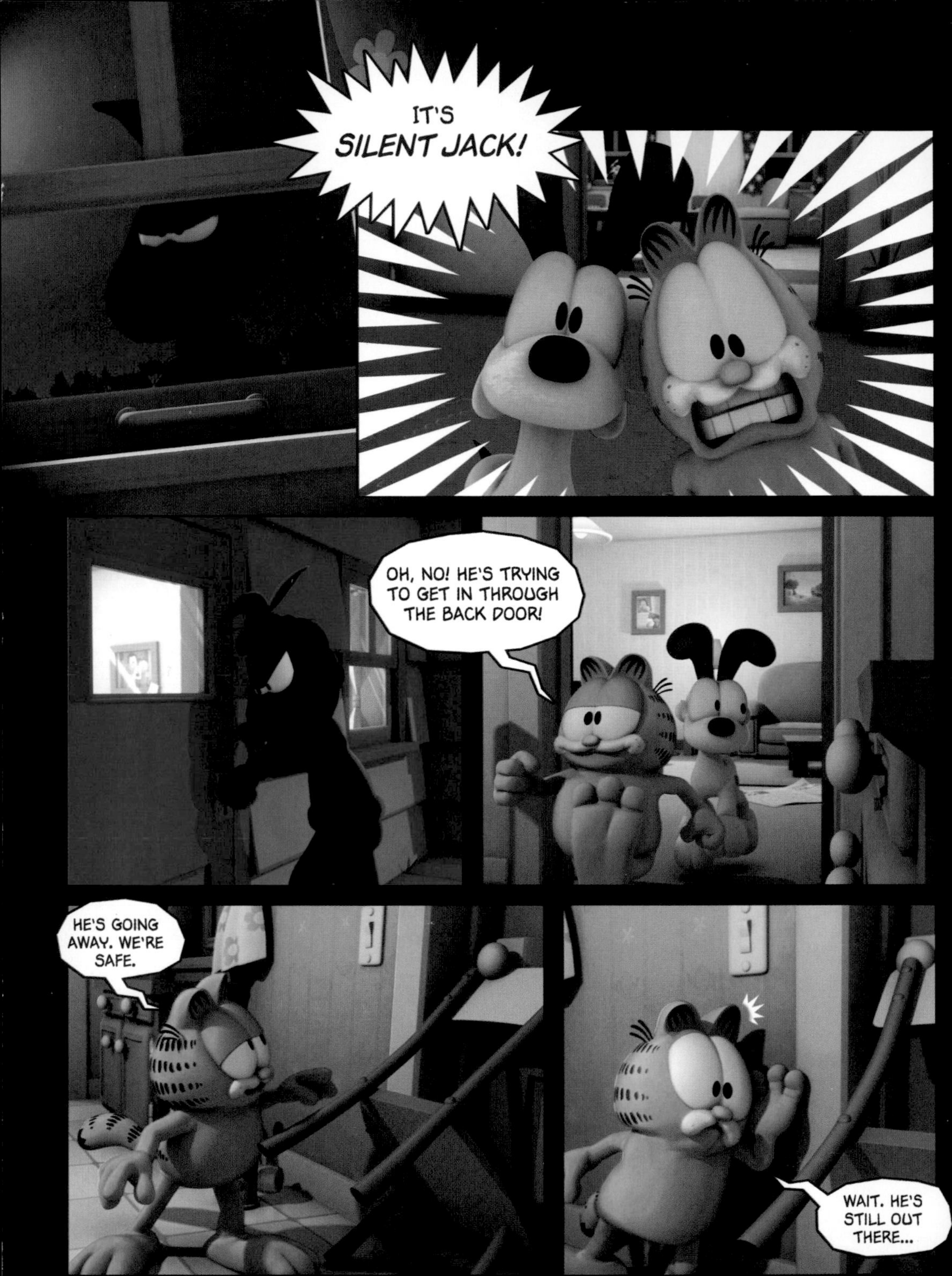
IT'S SILENT JACK!
OH, NO! HE'S TRYING TO GET IN THROUGH THE BACK DOOR!
HE'S GOING AWAY. WE'RE SAFE.
WAIT. HE'S STILL OUT THERE...

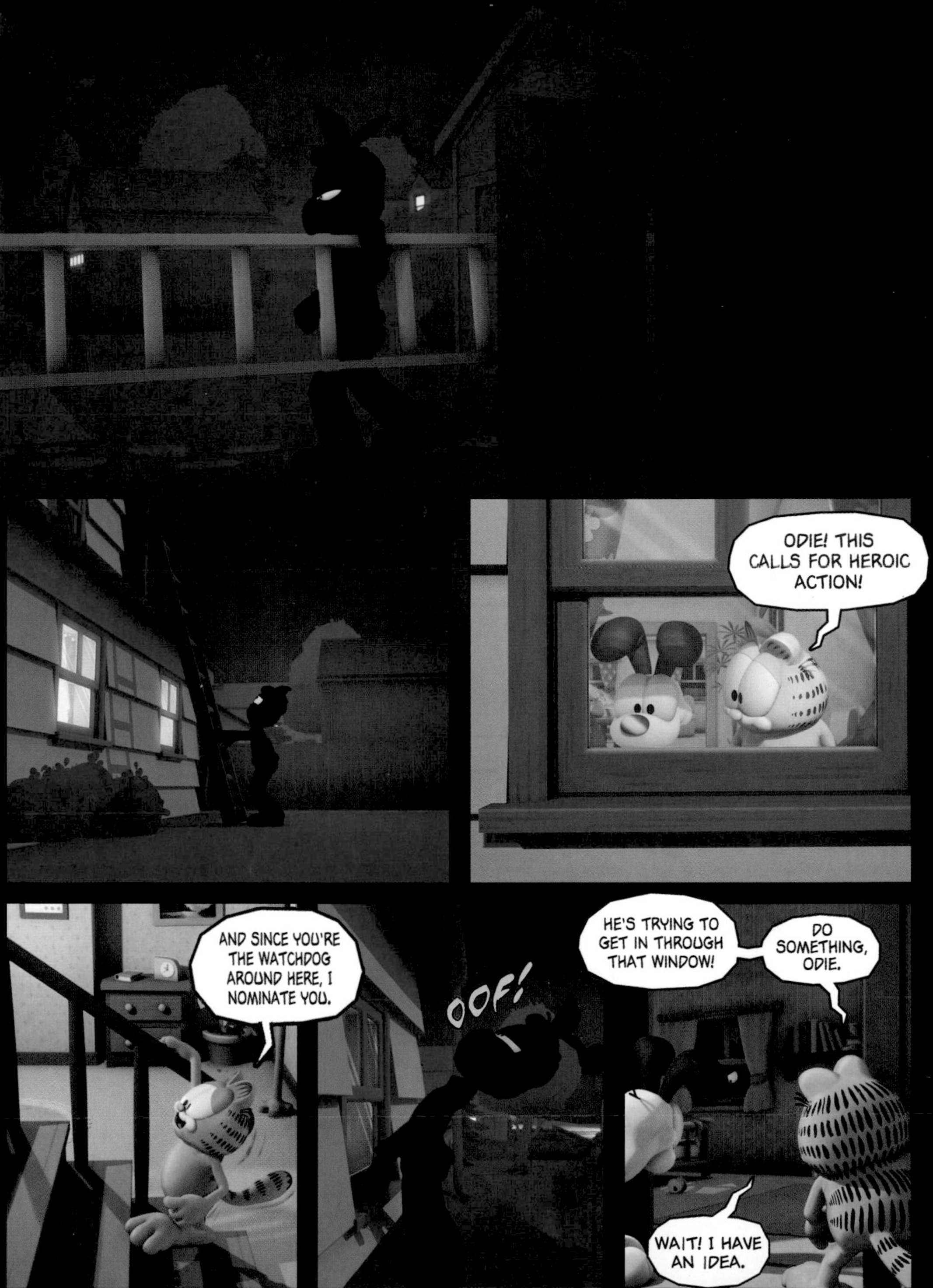
ODIE! THIS CALLS FOR HEROIC ACTION!
AND SINCE YOU'RE THE WATCHDOG AROUND HERE, I NOMINATE YOU.
OOF!
HE'S TRYING TO GET IN THROUGH THAT WINDOW!
DO SOMETHING, ODIE.
WAIT! I HAVE AN IDEA.

THIS OLD FAN!

JON STORED THIS UP HERE BECAUSE IT WAS TOO POWERFUL TO USE.

SQUEE

GLIK

?

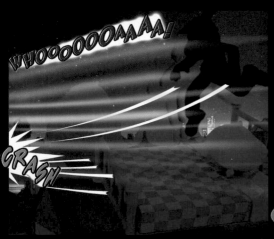

WHOOOOOOAAAAA!

CRASH

DON'T FEEL SORRY FOR HIM, ODIE!

SILENT JACK IS A DANGEROUS CRIMINAL. BUT WE GOT HIM.

CRASH

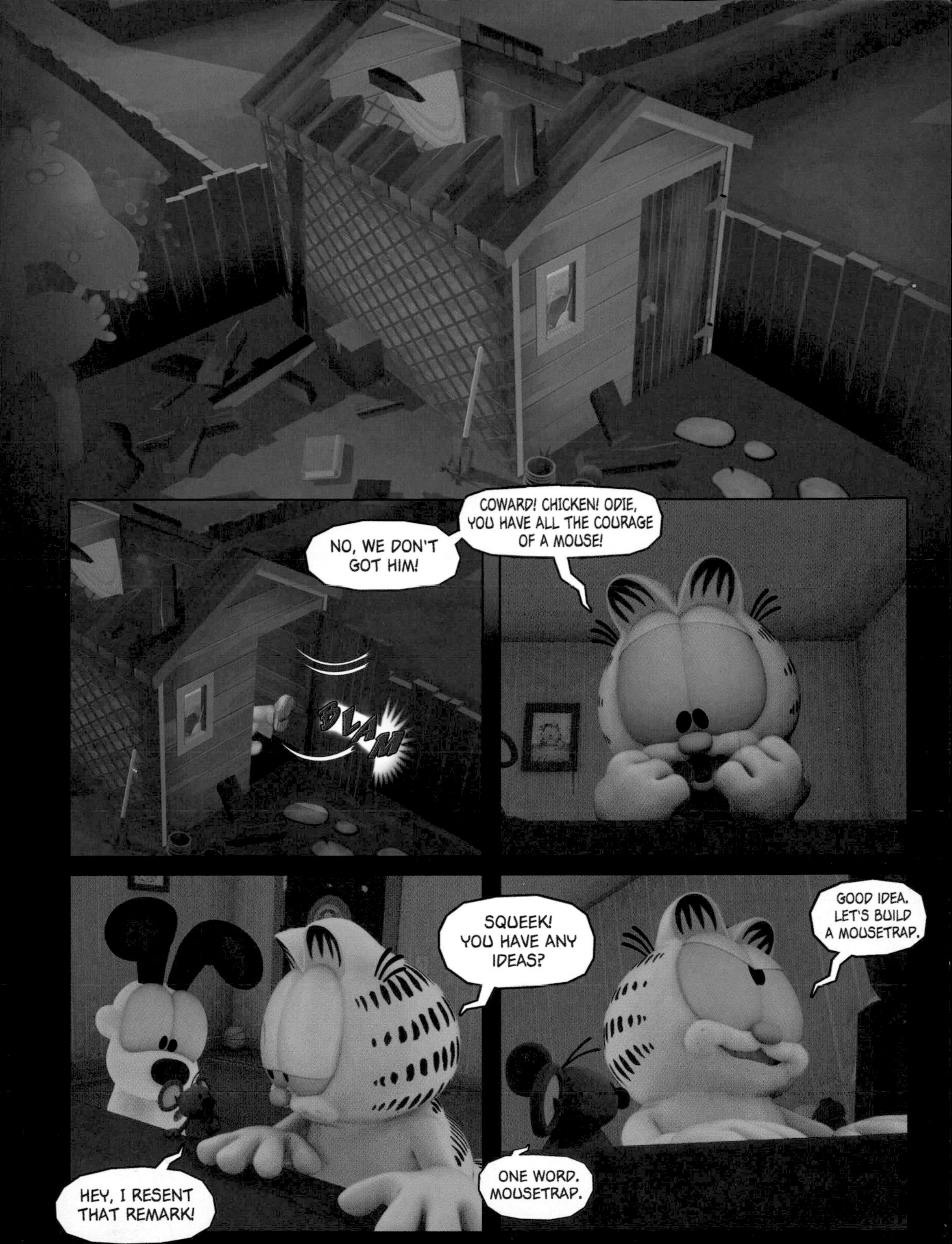
BLAM
NO, WE DON'T GOT HIM!
COWARD! CHICKEN! ODIE, YOU HAVE ALL THE COURAGE OF A MOUSE!
HEY, I RESENT THAT REMARK!
SQUEEK! YOU HAVE ANY IDEAS?
ONE WORD. MOUSETRAP.
GOOD IDEA. LET'S BUILD A MOUSETRAP.

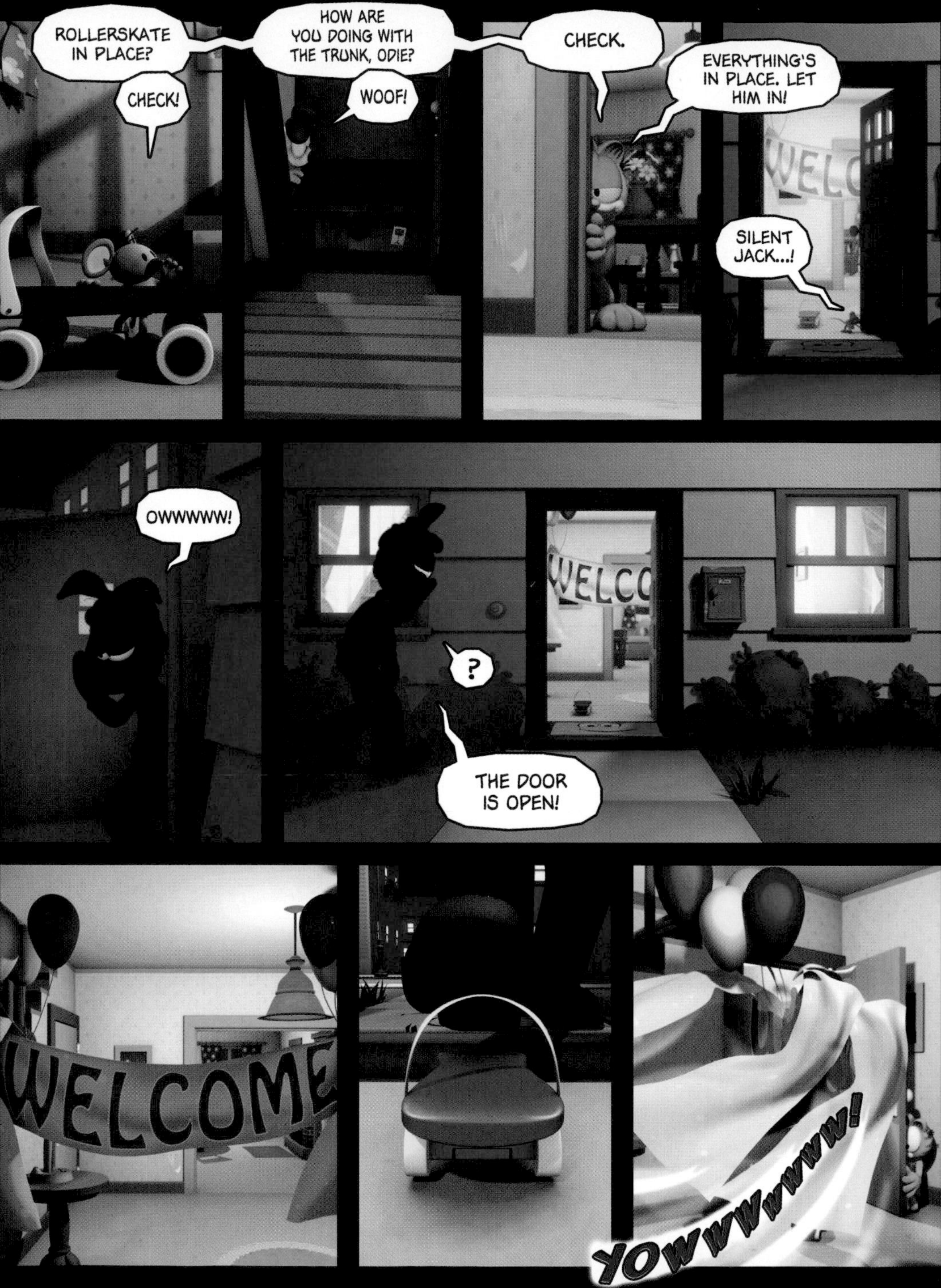
ROLLERSKATE IN PLACE?
CHECK!
HOW ARE YOU DOING WITH THE TRUNK, ODIE?
WOOF!
CHECK.
EVERYTHING'S IN PLACE. LET HIM IN!
WELC
SILENT JACK...!
OWWWWW!
WELCO
?
THE DOOR IS OPEN!
WELCOME
YOWWWwwww!

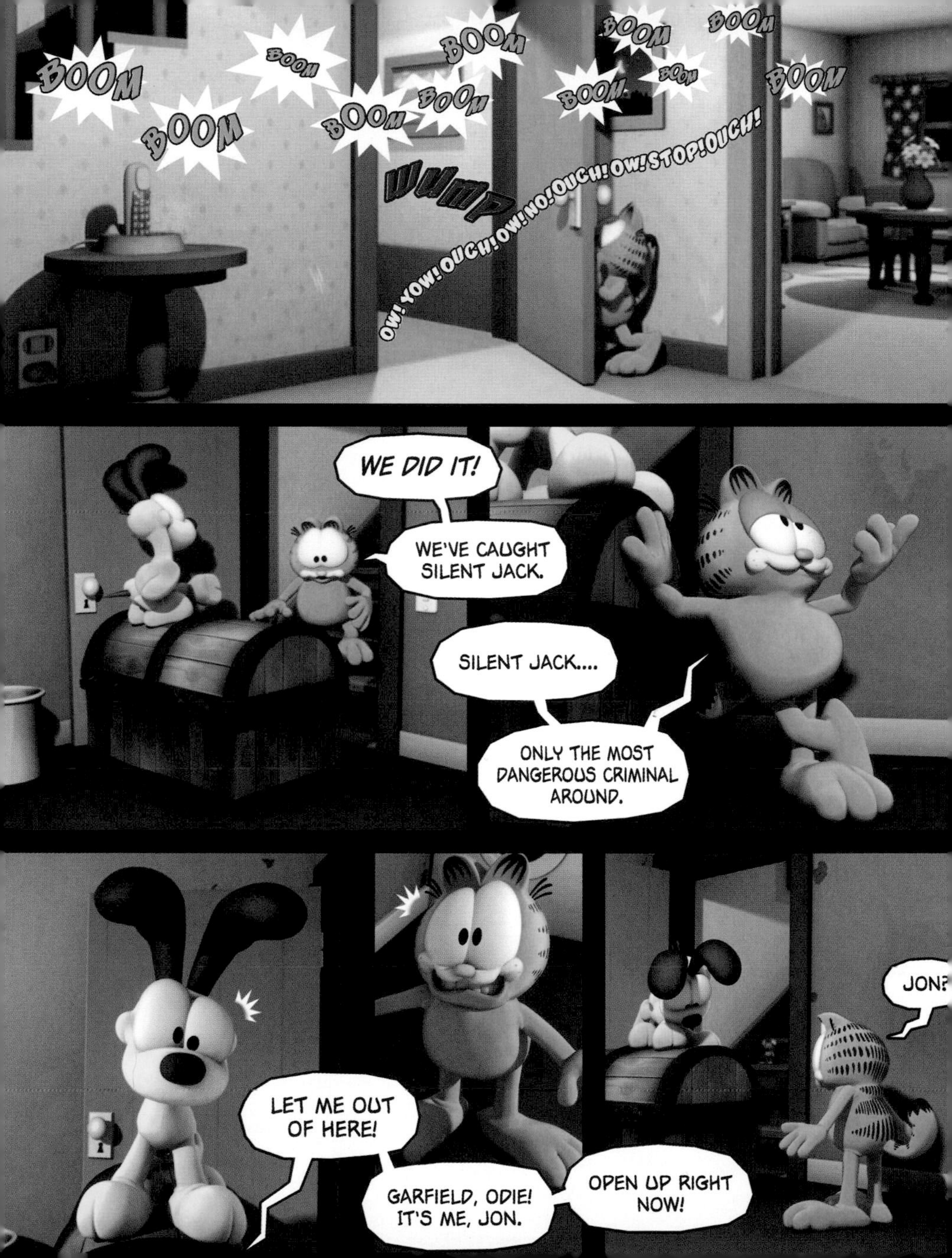
BOOM
BOOM
BOOM
BOOM
BOOM
BOOM
BOOM
BOOM
BOOM
BOOM
BOOM
WUMP
OW! YOW! OUCH! OW! NO! OUCH! OW! STOP! OUCH!
WE DID IT!
WE'VE CAUGHT SILENT JACK.
SILENT JACK....
ONLY THE MOST DANGEROUS CRIMINAL AROUND.
LET ME OUT OF HERE!
GARFIELD, ODIE! IT'S ME, JON.
OPEN UP RIGHT NOW!
JON?

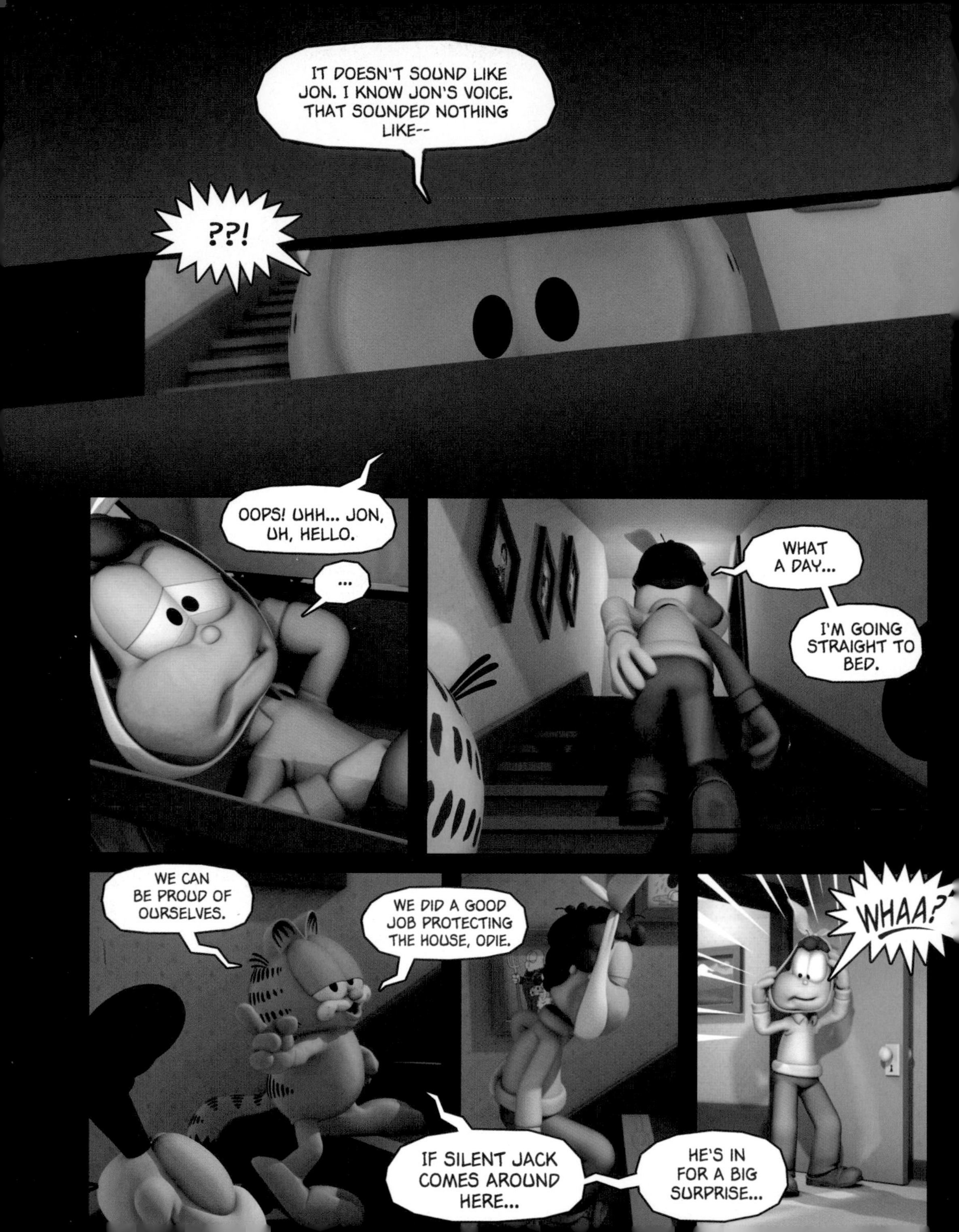
IT DOESN'T SOUND LIKE JON. I KNOW JON'S VOICE. THAT SOUNDED NOTHING LIKE--
??!
OOPS! UHH... JON, UH, HELLO.
...
WHAT A DAY...
I'M GOING STRAIGHT TO BED.
WE CAN BE PROUD OF OURSELVES.
WE DID A GOOD JOB PROTECTING THE HOUSE, ODIE.
IF SILENT JACK COMES AROUND HERE...
HE'S IN FOR A BIG SURPRISE...
WHAA?

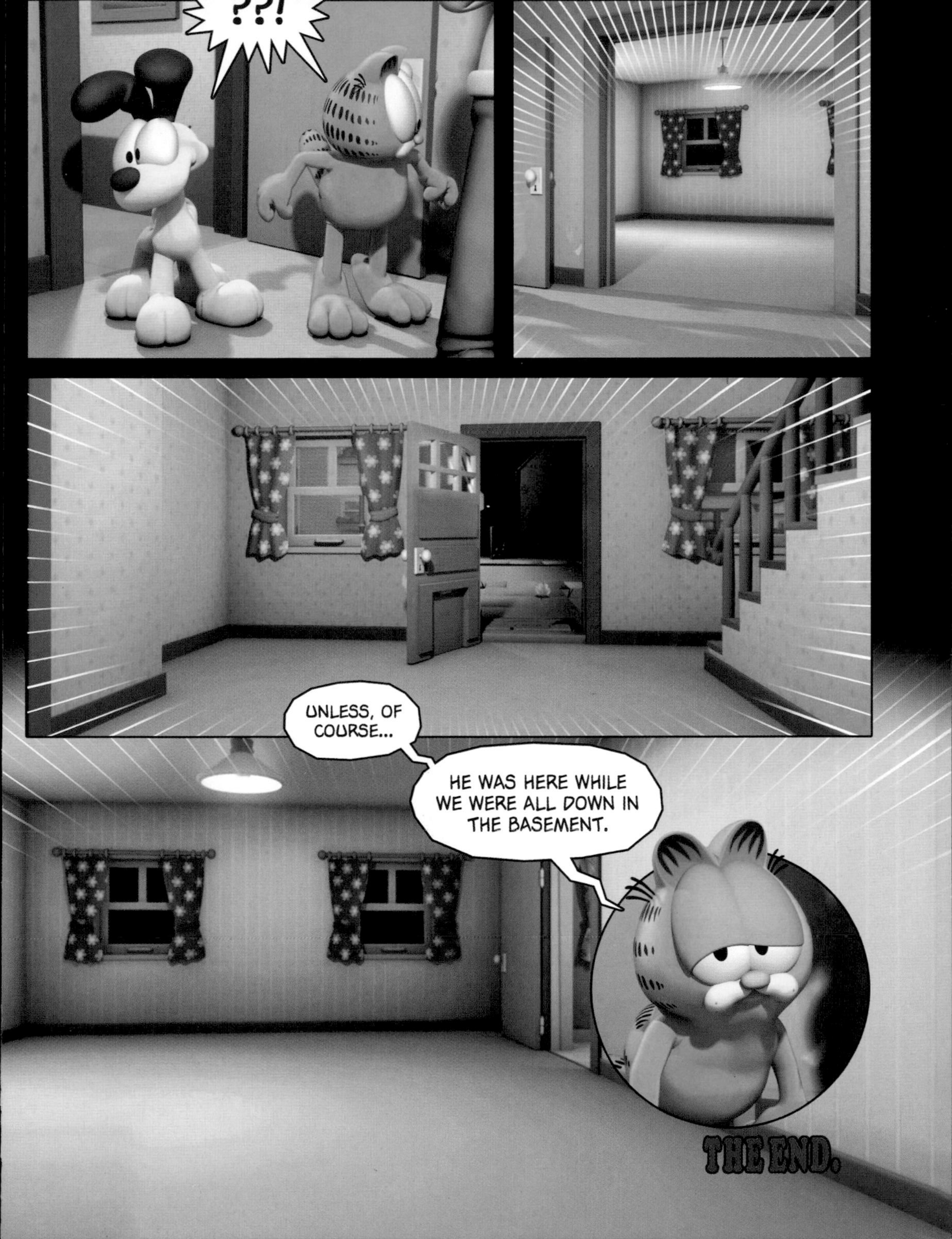
??!
UNLESS, OF COURSE...
HE WAS HERE WHILE WE WERE ALL DOWN IN THE BASEMENT.
THE END.

WATCH OUT FOR PAPERCUTZ™

Welcome to the pet-friendly fifth GARFIELD & Co graphic novel from Papercutz, the folks dedicated to publishing great graphic novels for all ages. I'm your Jon-like Editor-in-Chief, Jim Salicrup, with an extra-special surprise for you—a sneak peek at one of our latest and greatest new series of graphic novels DANCE CLASS #1 "So, You Think You Can Hip-Hop?"

DANCE CLASS, written by Béka and drawn by Crip, focuses on Julie, Lucy, and Alia, three best friends who all share one passion: dance! The three take classes at a local studio, with their frenemy, Carla; the only boy in class, Bruno; and Julie's little sister, Capucine. The classes include ballet, modern dance, and more, and are taught by Miss Anne, Miss Mary, and K.T.-- the handsome new hip-hop teacher the girls are all falling for!

Here's a short excerpt from DANCE CLASS #1 "So, You Think You Can Hip-Hop?":

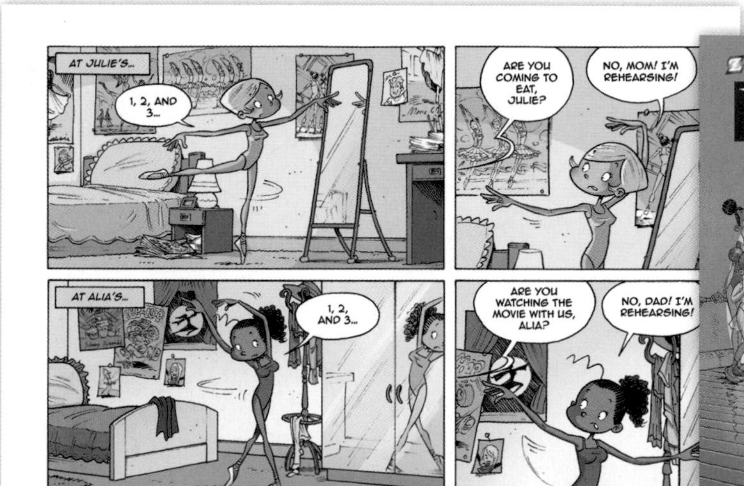

AT JULIE'S...
1, 2, AND 3...
ARE YOU COMING TO EAT, JULIE?
NO, MOM! I'M REHEARSING!
AT ALIA'S...
1, 2, AND 3...
ARE YOU WATCHING THE MOVIE WITH US, ALIA?
NO, DAD! I'M REHEARSING!
AT LUCIE'S...
GOODNIGHT, LUCIE!
GOOD-NIGHT!
I HOPE I GET THE MAIN ROLE IN "SLEEPING BEAUTY"! I PRACTICED ALL NIGHT!
ME, TOO!
ME, TOO!
I MOSTLY WORKED ON THE SCENE WHERE PRINCESS AURORA SLEEPS FOR A HUNDRED YEARS!
!
!

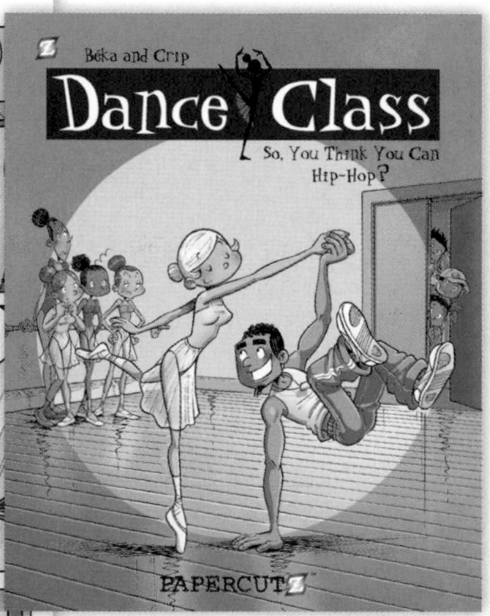

Béka and Crip
Dance Class
So, You Think You Can Hip-Hop?
PAPERCUTZ

Don't miss DANCE CLASS #1 "So, You Can Think You Can Hip-Hop" now on sale at booksellers everywhere!

So, as much as we hope you'll enjoy meeting the students of DANCE CLASS, we hope you don't forget about your friends in GARFIELD & Co! GARFIELD & Co #6 "Mother Garfield" is coming soon and I'm sure you don't want to miss it! Just as Garfield can never get enough lasagna, if you're like us, you can never get enough of Garfield either! Fortunately, more is on the way!

Jim

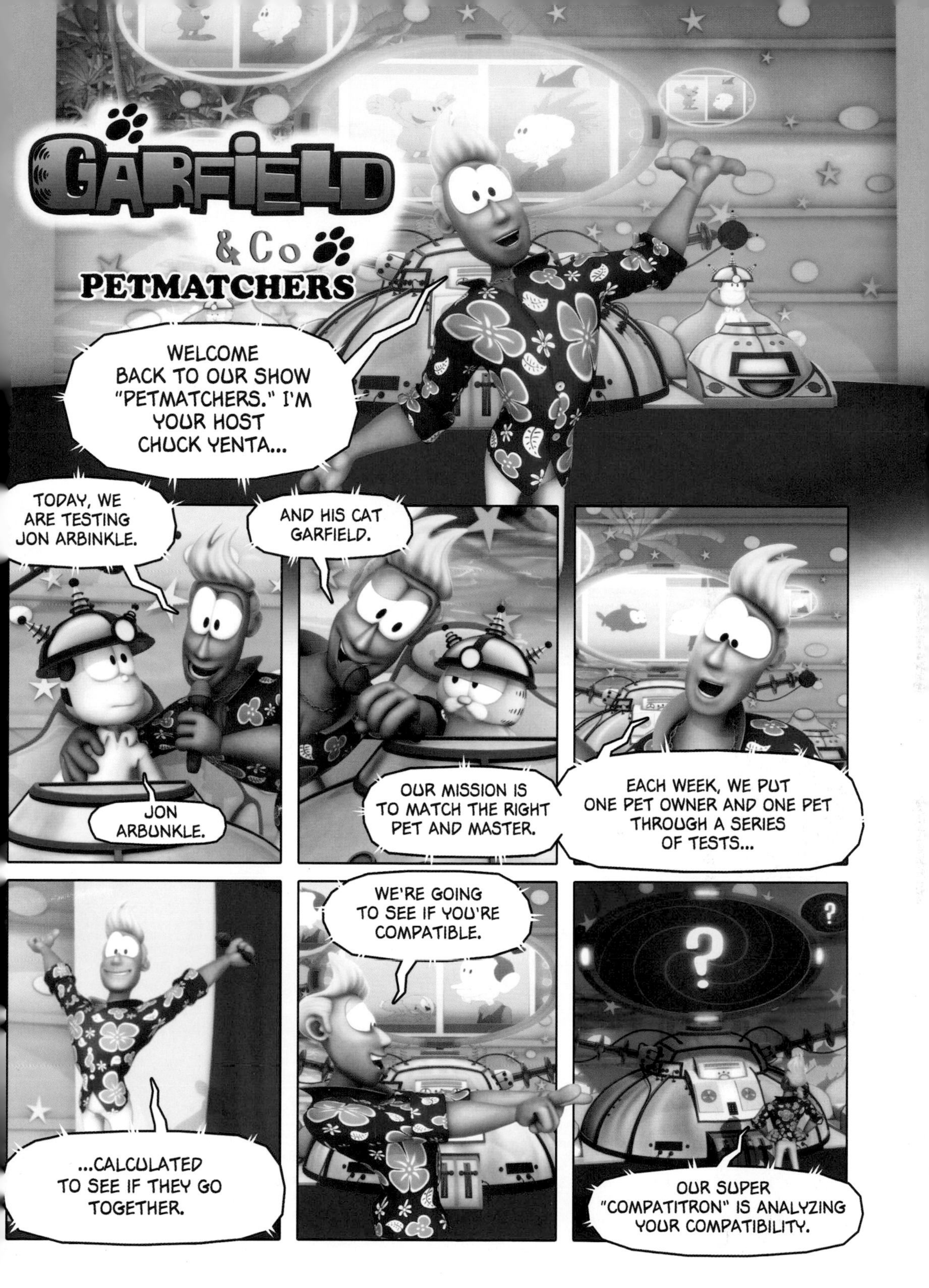
GARFIELD
& Co
PETMATCHERS
WELCOME BACK TO OUR SHOW "PETMATCHERS." I'M YOUR HOST CHUCK YENTA...
TODAY, WE ARE TESTING JON ARBINKLE.
JON ARBUNKLE.
AND HIS CAT GARFIELD.
OUR MISSION IS TO MATCH THE RIGHT PET AND MASTER.
EACH WEEK, WE PUT ONE PET OWNER AND ONE PET THROUGH A SERIES OF TESTS...
...CALCULATED TO SEE IF THEY GO TOGETHER.
WE'RE GOING TO SEE IF YOU'RE COMPATIBLE.
?
?
OUR SUPER "COMPATITRON" IS ANALYZING YOUR COMPATIBILITY.

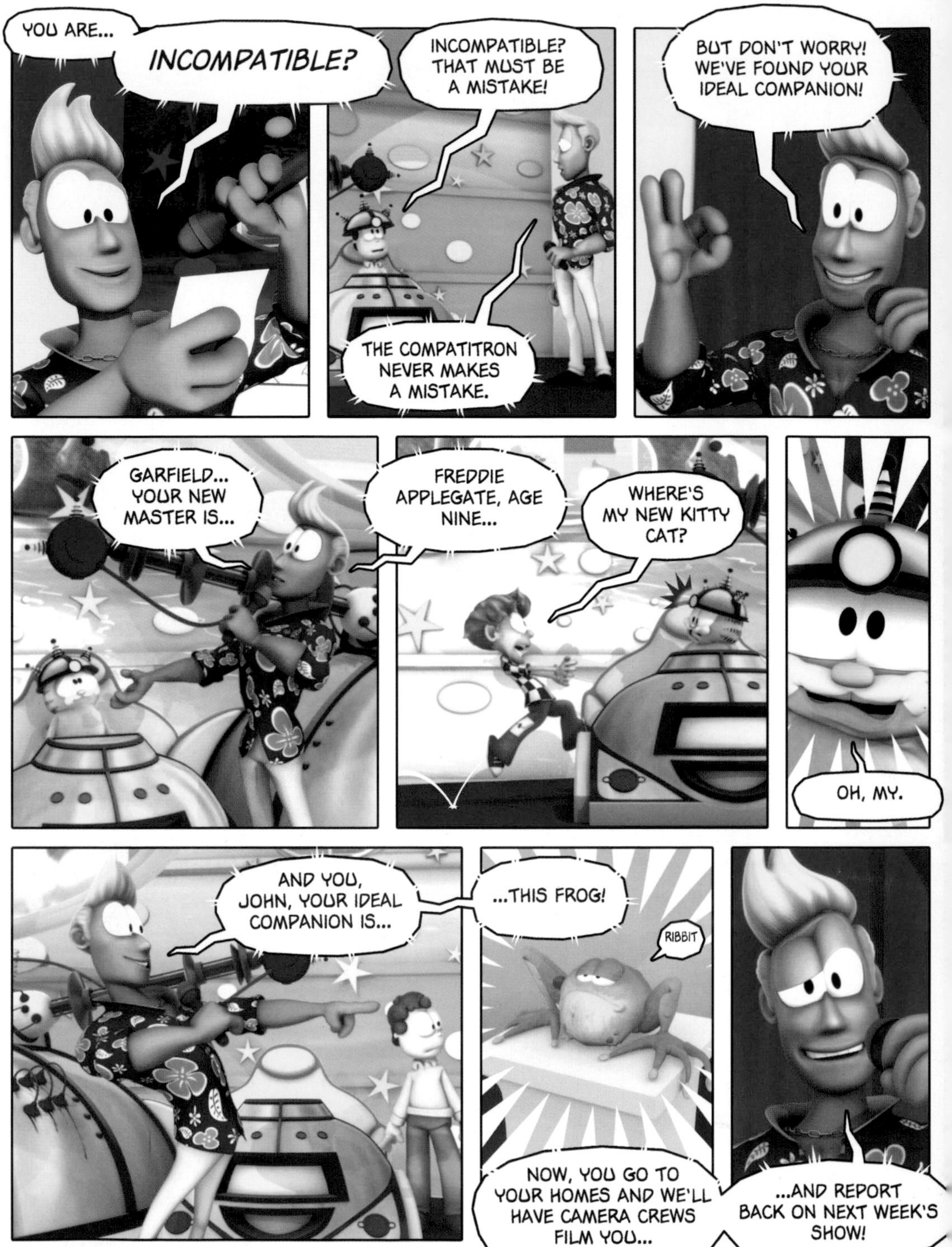
YOU ARE...
INCOMPATIBLE?
INCOMPATIBLE? THAT MUST BE A MISTAKE!
THE COMPATITRON NEVER MAKES A MISTAKE.
BUT DON'T WORRY! WE'VE FOUND YOUR IDEAL COMPANION!
GARFIELD... YOUR NEW MASTER IS...
FREDDIE APPLEGATE, AGE NINE...
WHERE'S MY NEW KITTY CAT?
OH, MY.
AND YOU, JOHN, YOUR IDEAL COMPANION IS...
...THIS FROG!
RIBBIT
NOW, YOU GO TO YOUR HOMES AND WE'LL HAVE CAMERA CREWS FILM YOU...
...AND REPORT BACK ON NEXT WEEK'S SHOW!

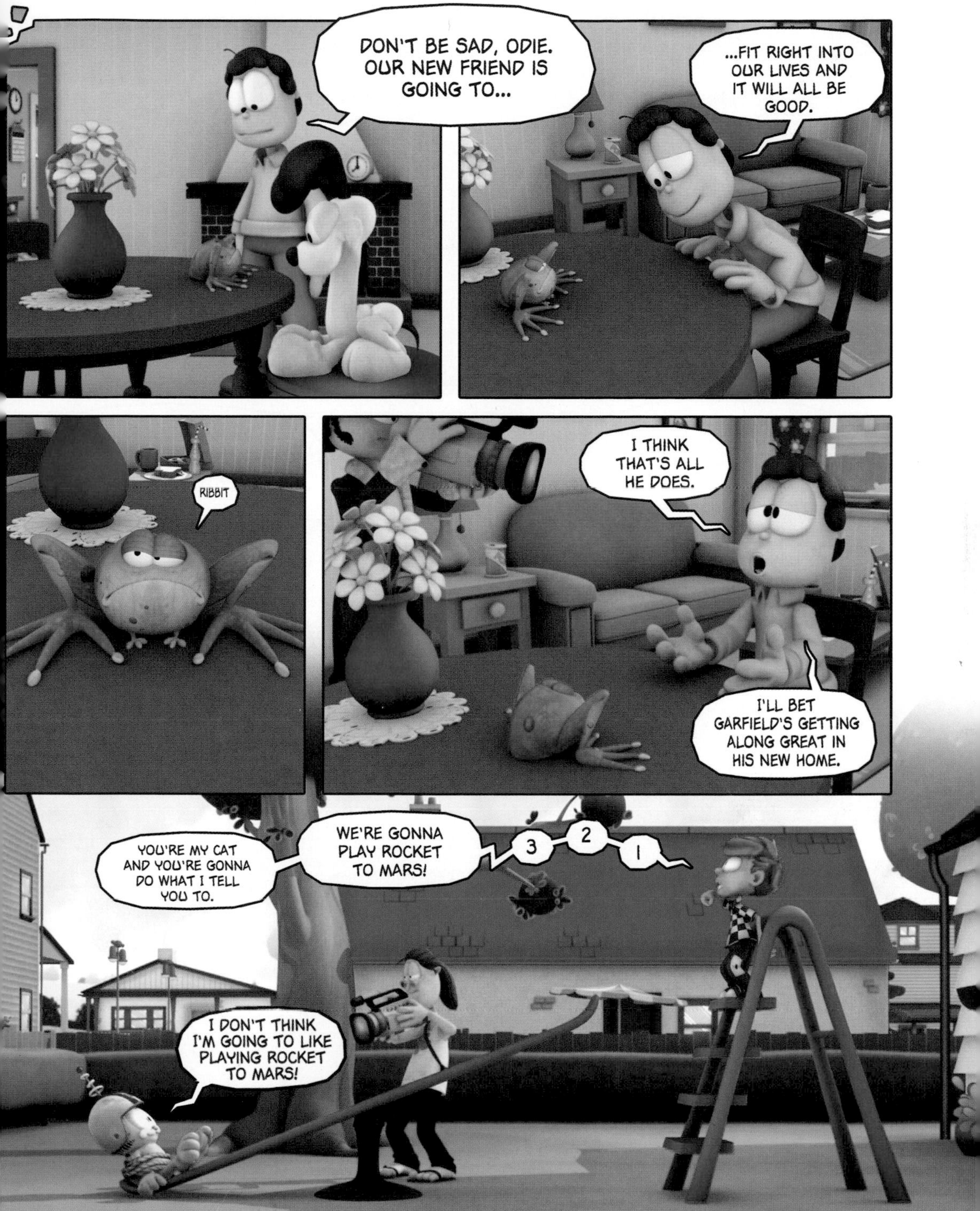

DON'T BE SAD, ODIE. OUR NEW FRIEND IS GOING TO...
...FIT RIGHT INTO OUR LIVES AND IT WILL ALL BE GOOD.
RIBBIT
I THINK THAT'S ALL HE DOES.
I'LL BET GARFIELD'S GETTING ALONG GREAT IN HIS NEW HOME.
YOU'RE MY CAT AND YOU'RE GONNA DO WHAT I TELL YOU TO.
WE'RE GONNA PLAY ROCKET TO MARS!
3
2
1
I DON'T THINK I'M GOING TO LIKE PLAYING ROCKET TO MARS!

AAAAAAAAAAAAAAAAAAAAAAA
SPROING
WUMP
AAAAAAAAAAAA
AAAAAAAAAA
CRASH
I WAS RIGHT. I DON'T LIKE PLAYING ROCKET TO MARS!
NOW HE WANTS TO PLAY COPS AND ROBBERS, AND I HAVE TO BE THE ROBBER.
THIS CAN ONLY END BAD...
OH! WHERE IS THAT BAD KITTY CAT BURGLAR?
I'M GOING TO ARREST HIM...
...AND MAKE SURE HE GETS THE ULTIMATE PUNISHMENT.
THIS IS THE ULTIMATE PUNISHMENT.
??

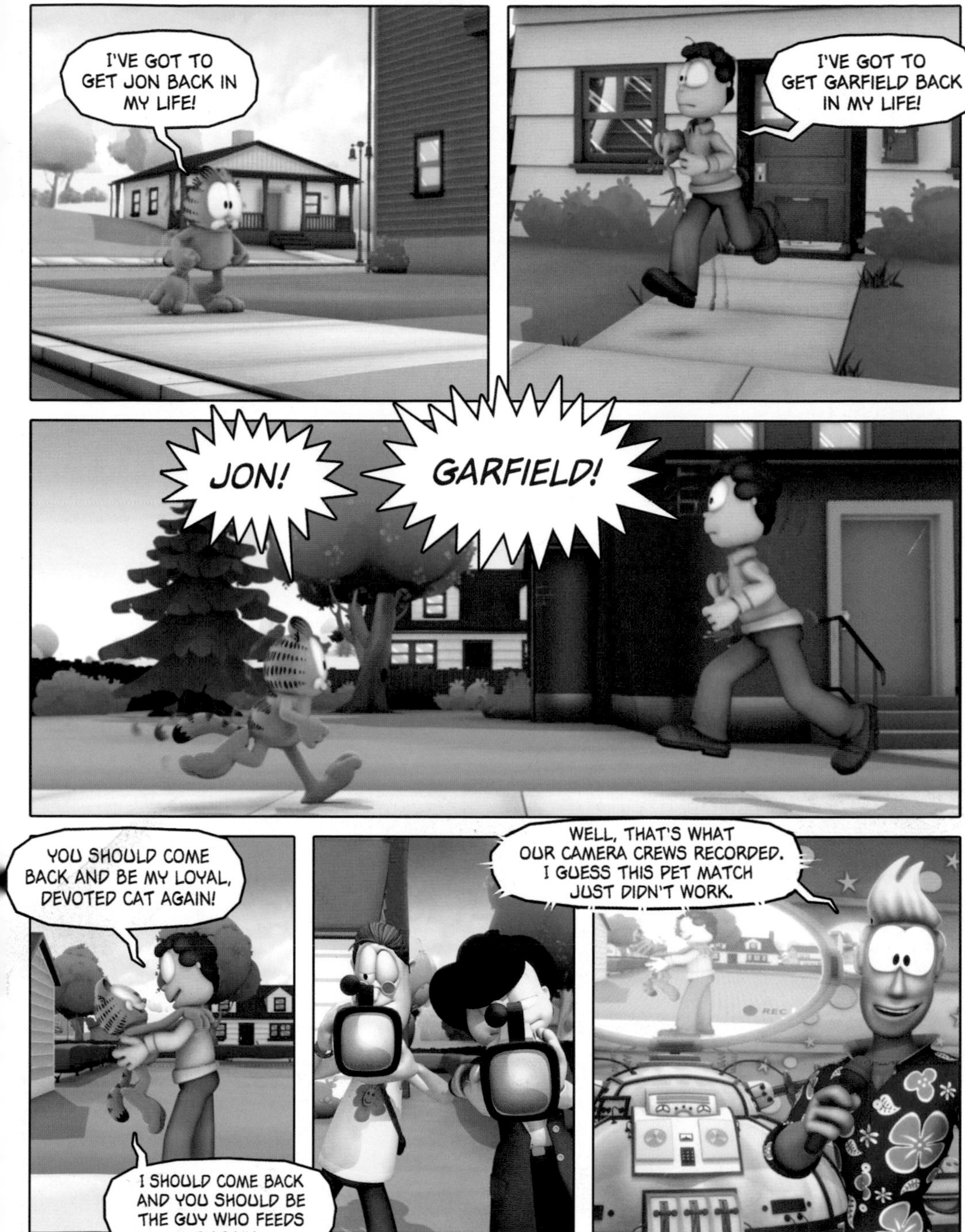
I'VE GOT TO GET JON BACK IN MY LIFE!
I'VE GOT TO GET GARFIELD BACK IN MY LIFE!
JON!
GARFIELD!
YOU SHOULD COME BACK AND BE MY LOYAL, DEVOTED CAT AGAIN!
I SHOULD COME BACK AND YOU SHOULD BE THE GUY WHO FEEDS ME AGAIN.
WELL, THAT'S WHAT OUR CAMERA CREWS RECORDED. I GUESS THIS PET MATCH JUST DIDN'T WORK.

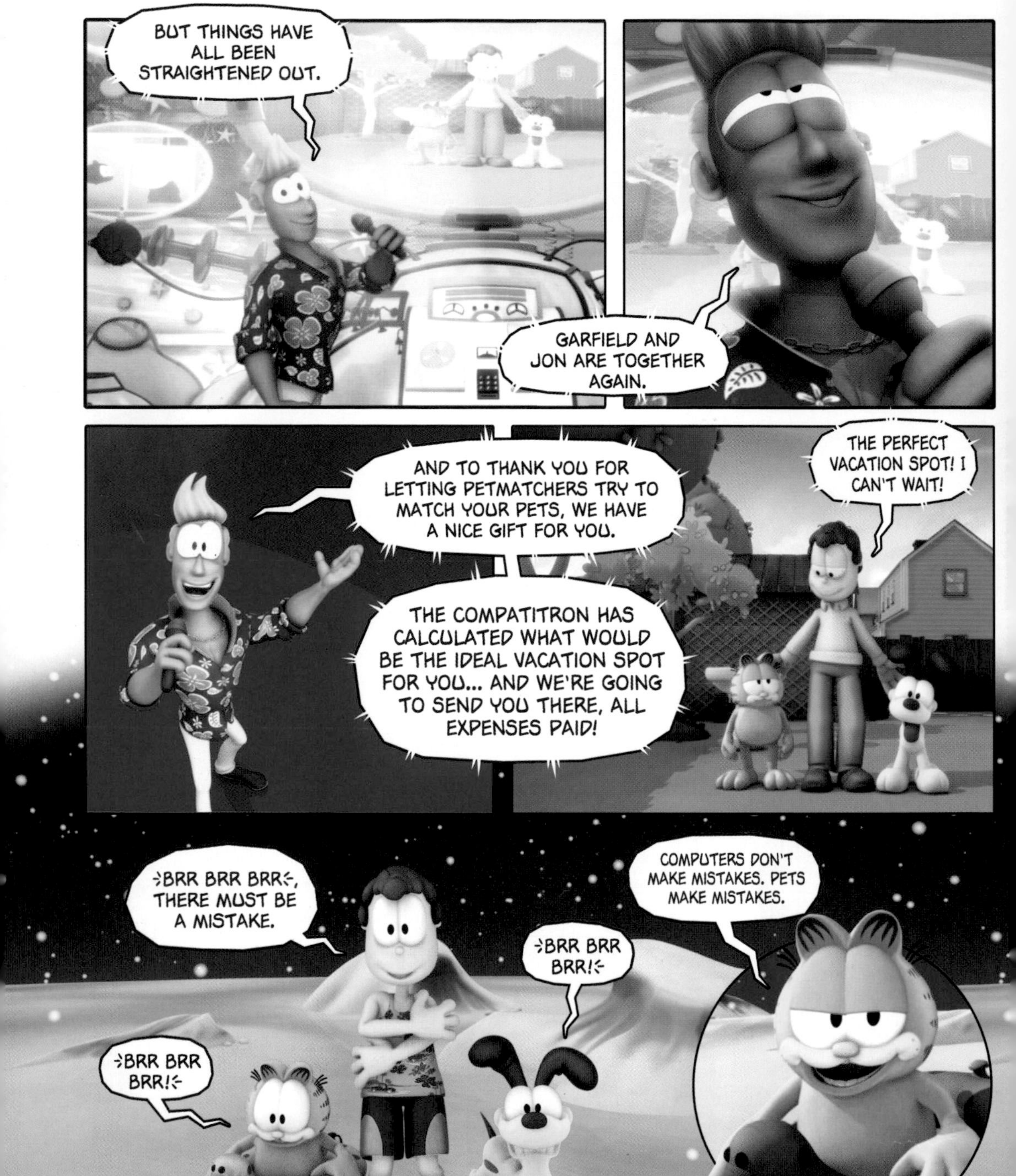
BUT THINGS HAVE ALL BEEN STRAIGHTENED OUT.
GARFIELD AND JON ARE TOGETHER AGAIN.
AND TO THANK YOU FOR LETTING PETMATCHERS TRY TO MATCH YOUR PETS, WE HAVE A NICE GIFT FOR YOU.
THE COMPATITRON HAS CALCULATED WHAT WOULD BE THE IDEAL VACATION SPOT FOR YOU... AND WE'RE GOING TO SEND YOU THERE, ALL EXPENSES PAID!
THE PERFECT VACATION SPOT! I CAN'T WAIT!
BRR BRR BRR, THERE MUST BE A MISTAKE.
BRR BRR BRR!
BRR BRR BRR!
COMPUTERS DON'T MAKE MISTAKES. PETS MAKE MISTAKES.
THE END.

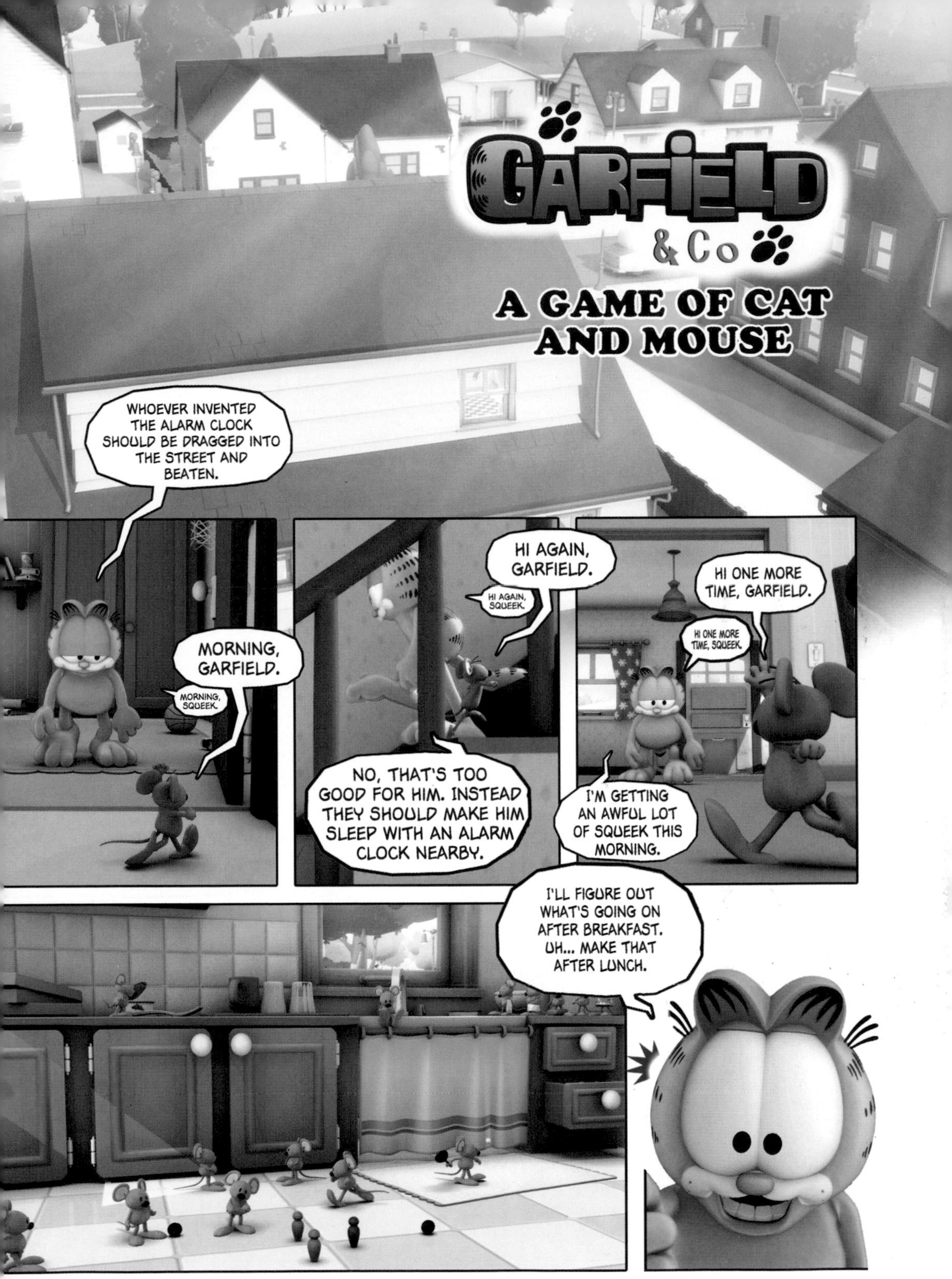

GARFIELD
& Co
A GAME OF CAT AND MOUSE
WHOEVER INVENTED THE ALARM CLOCK SHOULD BE DRAGGED INTO THE STREET AND BEATEN.
MORNING, GARFIELD.
MORNING, SQUEEK.
HI AGAIN, GARFIELD.
HI AGAIN, SQUEEK.
NO, THAT'S TOO GOOD FOR HIM. INSTEAD THEY SHOULD MAKE HIM SLEEP WITH AN ALARM CLOCK NEARBY.
HI ONE MORE TIME, GARFIELD.
HI ONE MORE TIME, SQUEEK.
I'M GETTING AN AWFUL LOT OF SQUEEK THIS MORNING.
I'LL FIGURE OUT WHAT'S GOING ON AFTER BREAKFAST. UH... MAKE THAT AFTER LUNCH.

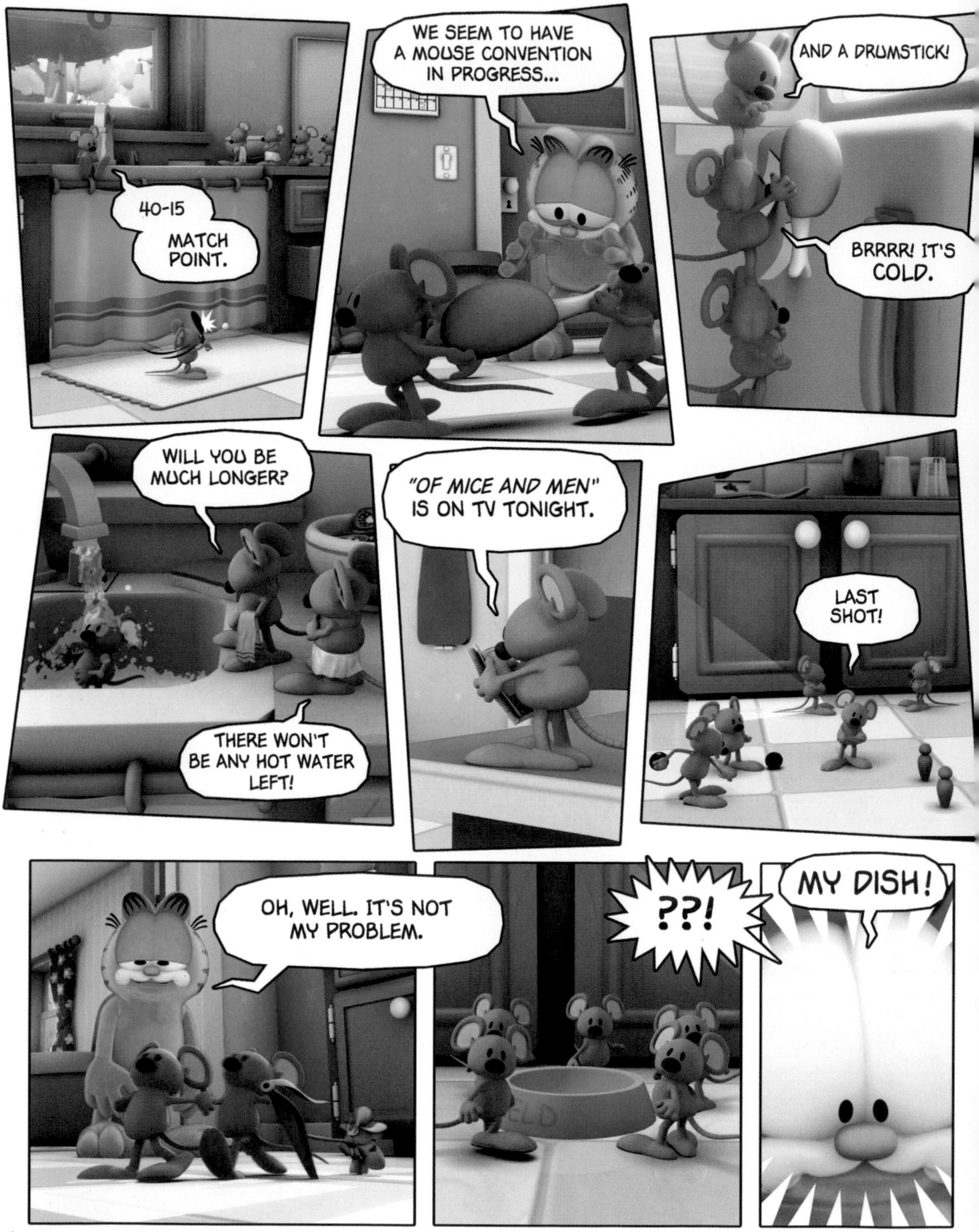
40-15
MATCH POINT.
WE SEEM TO HAVE A MOUSE CONVENTION IN PROGRESS...
AND A DRUMSTICK!
BRRRR! IT'S COLD.
WILL YOU BE MUCH LONGER?
THERE WON'T BE ANY HOT WATER LEFT!
"OF MICE AND MEN" IS ON TV TONIGHT.
LAST SHOT!
OH, WELL. IT'S NOT MY PROBLEM.
??!
MY DISH!

THIS IS MY PROBLEM!

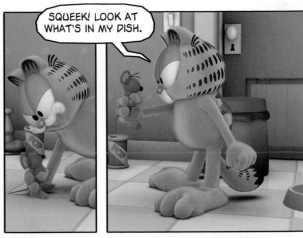

SQUEEK! LOOK AT WHAT'S IN MY DISH.

THERE'S NOTHING IN YOUR DISH.

MY POINT, EXACTLY.

ALL THESE MICE... MY COUSINS AND UNCLES AND NEPHEWS...

...THEY HAD NO PLACE ELSE TO GO.

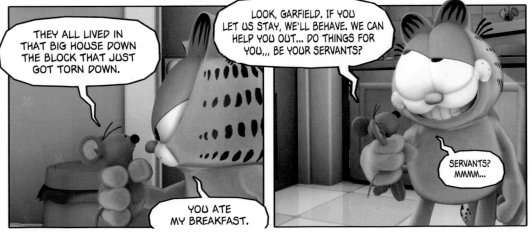

THEY ALL LIVED IN THAT BIG HOUSE DOWN THE BLOCK THAT JUST GOT TORN DOWN.

YOU ATE MY BREAKFAST.

LOOK, GARFIELD. IF YOU LET US STAY, WE'LL BEHAVE. WE CAN HELP YOU OUT... DO THINGS FOR YOU,,, BE YOUR SERVANTS?

SERVANTS? MMMM...

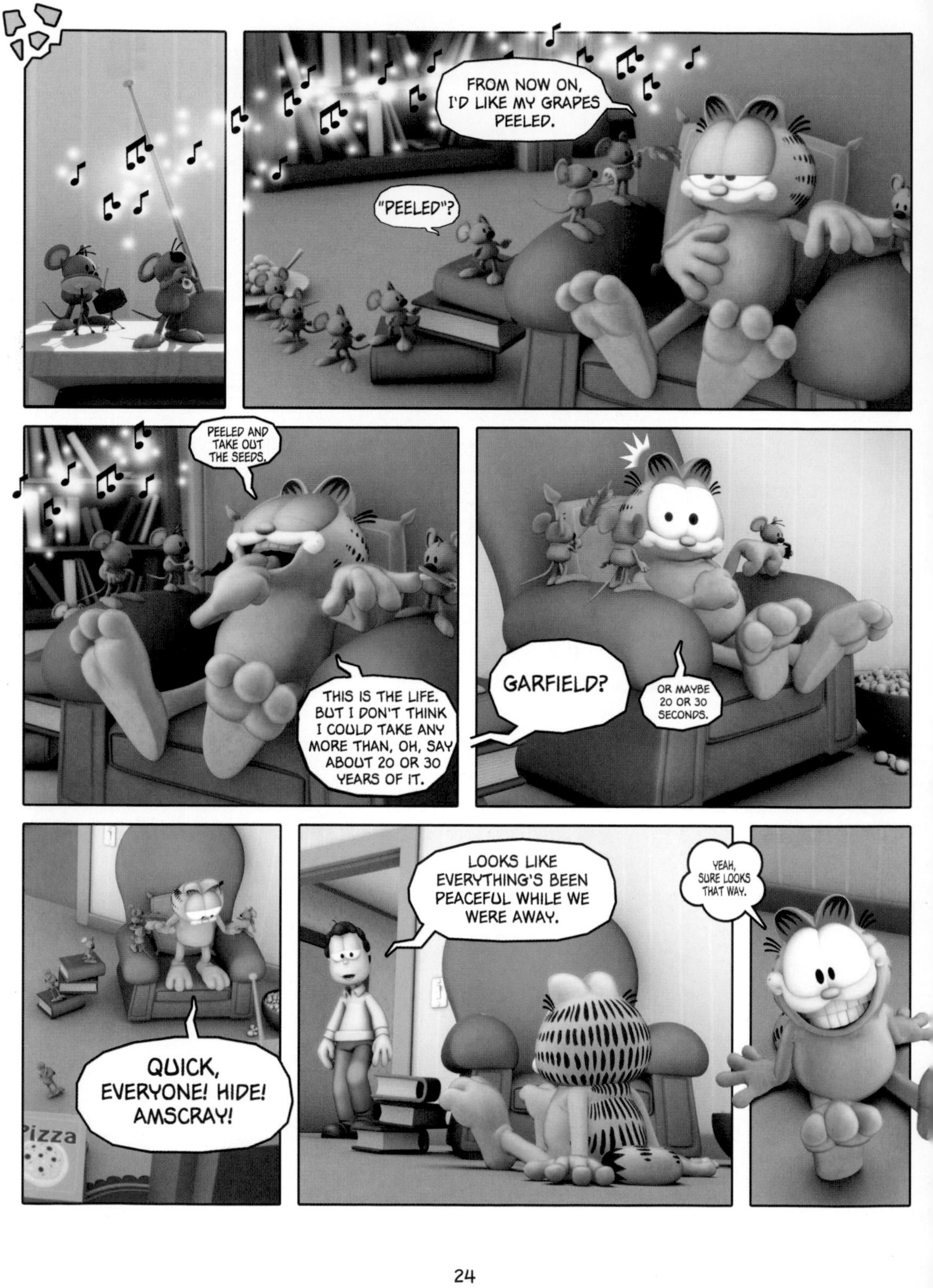
FROM NOW ON, I'D LIKE MY GRAPES PEELED.
"PEELED"?
PEELED AND TAKE OUT THE SEEDS.
THIS IS THE LIFE. BUT I DON'T THINK I COULD TAKE ANY MORE THAN, OH, SAY ABOUT 20 OR 30 YEARS OF IT.
GARFIELD?
OR MAYBE 20 OR 30 SECONDS.
QUICK, EVERYONE! HIDE! AMSCRAY!
Pizza
LOOKS LIKE EVERYTHING'S BEEN PEACEFUL WHILE WE WERE AWAY.
YEAH, SURE LOOKS THAT WAY.

WHEN I'M AWAY, I ALWAYS FEEL SECURE KNOWING YOU'RE WATCHING THE HOUSE, GARFIELD.

I FEEL GOOD WHEN YOU'RE AWAY, TOO.

I KNOW THERE WON'T BE ANY INTRUDERS OR ACCIDENTS... OR MICE.

ESPECIALLY MICE.

AAAAH... BUT FIRST SOMETHING TO EAT!

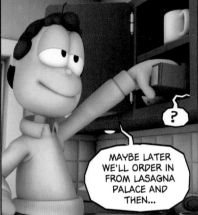

MAYBE LATER WE'LL ORDER IN FROM LASAGNA PALACE AND THEN...

?

GARFIELD SAID WE SHOULD HIDE.

WE BETTER GET OUTTA HERE.

?

I HAVE MICE IN MY CUPBOARD!

25

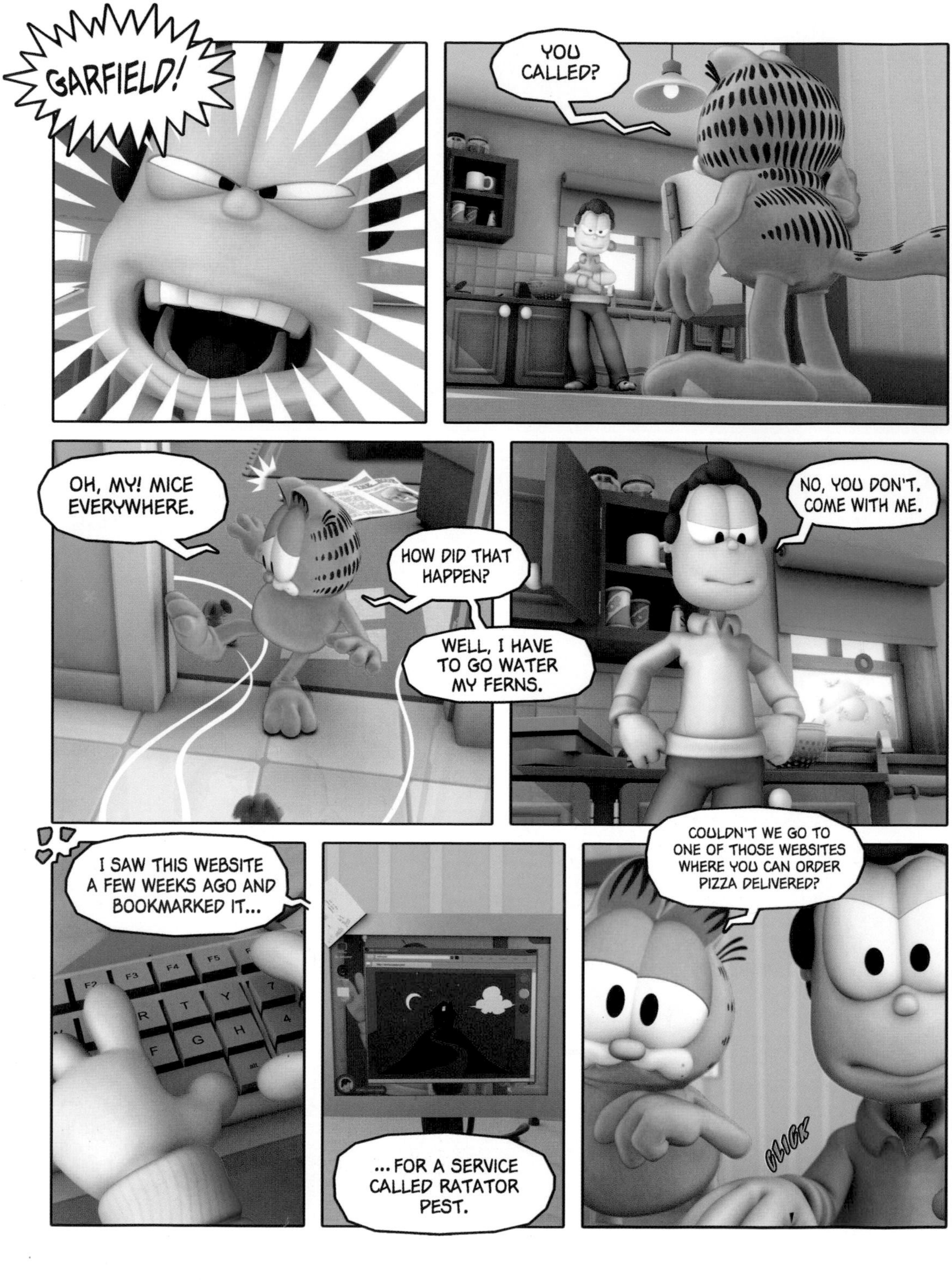
GARFIELD!
YOU CALLED?
OH, MY! MICE EVERYWHERE.
HOW DID THAT HAPPEN?
WELL, I HAVE TO GO WATER MY FERNS.
NO, YOU DON'T. COME WITH ME.
I SAW THIS WEBSITE A FEW WEEKS AGO AND BOOKMARKED IT...
...FOR A SERVICE CALLED RATATOR PEST.
COULDN'T WE GO TO ONE OF THOSE WEBSITES WHERE YOU CAN ORDER PIZZA DELIVERED?
CLICK

MOUSE PROBLEM IN YOUR HOUSE?

THEN CALL RATATOR PEST!

OUR TRAINED SPECIALISTS WILL RUSH TO YOUR HOME...

...WHERE THEY WILL STOP AT NOTHING...

RATATOR PEST. A MOUSE'S WORST NIGHTMARE.

CLICK HERE TO ORDER OUR SERVICE.

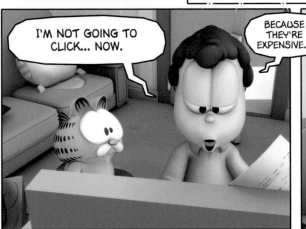

I'M NOT GOING TO CLICK... NOW.

BECAUSE THEY'RE EXPENSIVE...

...AND GETTING RID OF MICE IS YOUR JOB.

I MEAN, YOU ARE THE CAT AROUND HERE.

YOU ARE GOING TO GET RID OF THESE MICE. EVERY LAST ONE OF THEM.

I'M GOING OUT FOR A WHILE. IF THERE'S A SINGLE MOUSE HERE WHEN I GET BACK...

I'M CALLING IN RATATOR PEST.

AND I'M DEDUCTING THE COST OF THEM FROM MY CAT FOOD BUDGET. YOU WON'T SEE LASAGNA IN THIS HOUSE FOR YEARS.

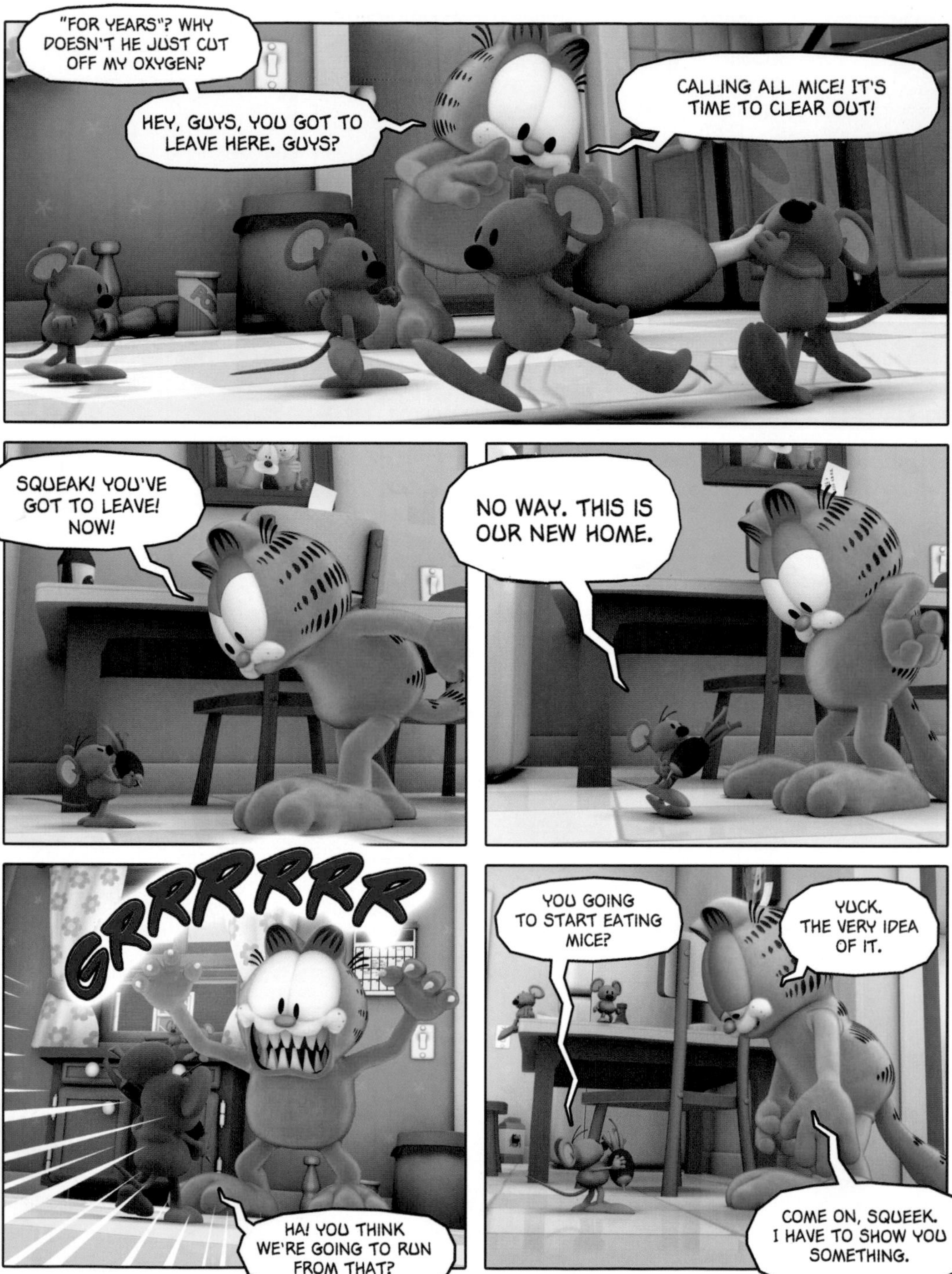
"FOR YEARS"? WHY DOESN'T HE JUST CUT OFF MY OXYGEN?
HEY, GUYS, YOU GOT TO LEAVE HERE. GUYS?
CALLING ALL MICE! IT'S TIME TO CLEAR OUT!
SQUEAK! YOU'VE GOT TO LEAVE! NOW!
NO WAY. THIS IS OUR NEW HOME.
GRRRRRRR
HA! YOU THINK WE'RE GOING TO RUN FROM THAT?
YOU GOING TO START EATING MICE?
YUCK. THE VERY IDEA OF IT.
COME ON, SQUEEK. I HAVE TO SHOW YOU SOMETHING.

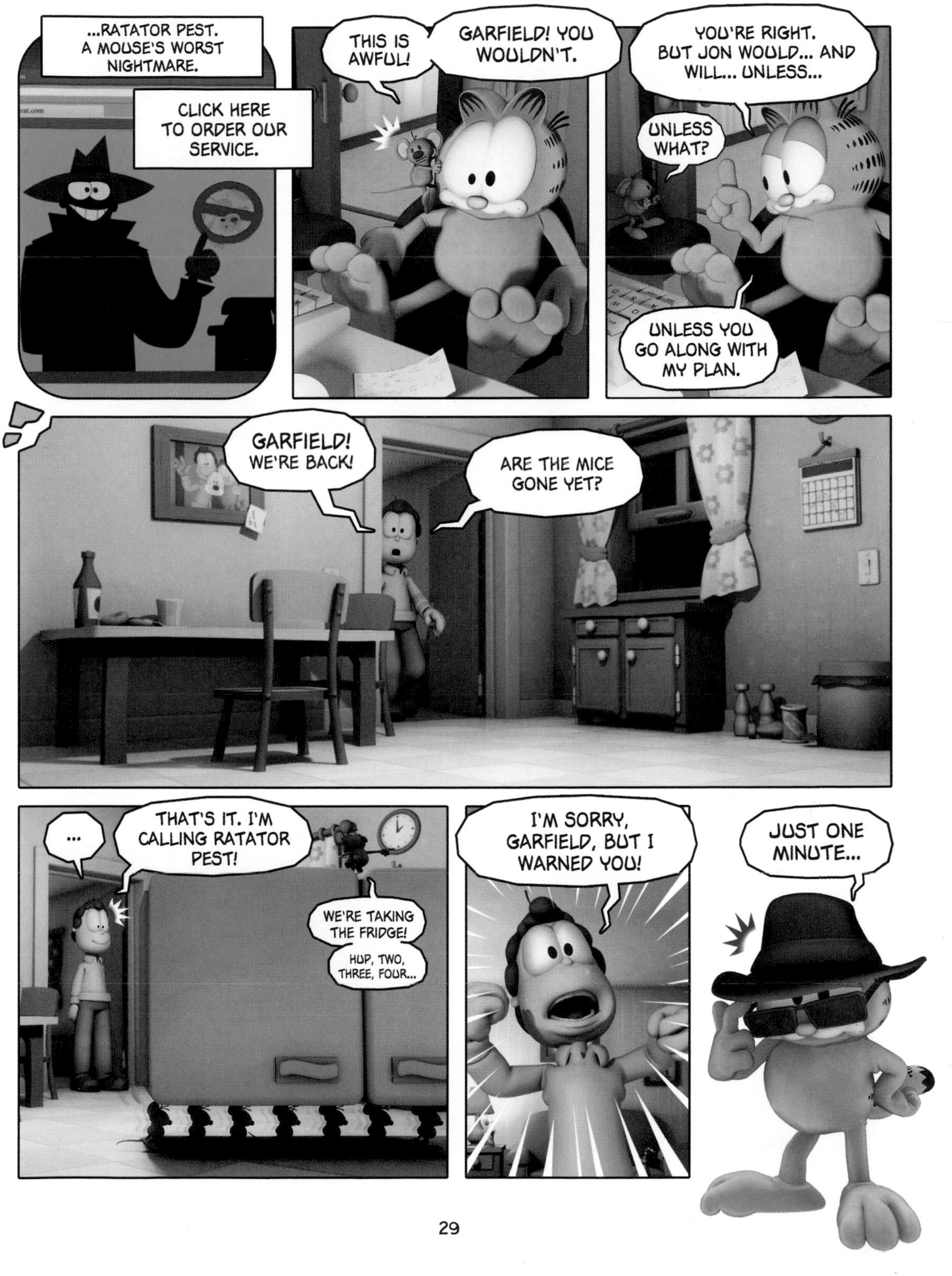
...RATATOR PEST. A MOUSE'S WORST NIGHTMARE.
CLICK HERE TO ORDER OUR SERVICE.
THIS IS AWFUL!
GARFIELD! YOU WOULDN'T.
YOU'RE RIGHT. BUT JON WOULD... AND WILL... UNLESS...
UNLESS WHAT?
UNLESS YOU GO ALONG WITH MY PLAN.
GARFIELD! WE'RE BACK!
ARE THE MICE GONE YET?
...
THAT'S IT. I'M CALLING RATATOR PEST!
WE'RE TAKING THE FRIDGE!
HUP, TWO, THREE, FOUR...
I'M SORRY, GARFIELD, BUT I WARNED YOU!
JUST ONE MINUTE...

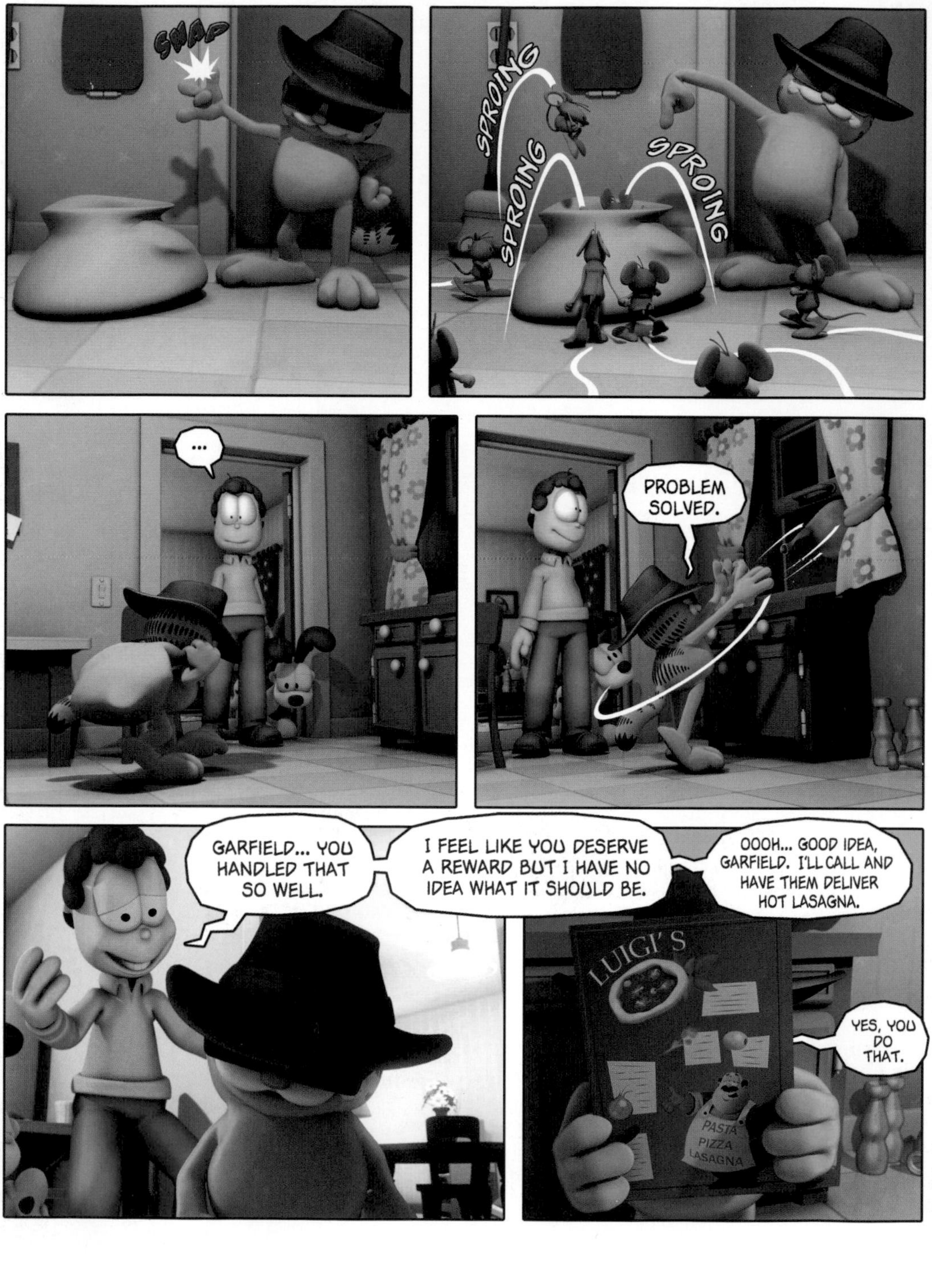
SNAP
SPROING
SPROING
SPROING
SPROING
...
PROBLEM SOLVED.
GARFIELD... YOU HANDLED THAT SO WELL.
I FEEL LIKE YOU DESERVE A REWARD BUT I HAVE NO IDEA WHAT IT SHOULD BE.
OOOH... GOOD IDEA, GARFIELD. I'LL CALL AND HAVE THEM DELIVER HOT LASAGNA.
LUIGI'S
PASTA
PIZZA
LASAGNA
YES, YOU DO THAT.

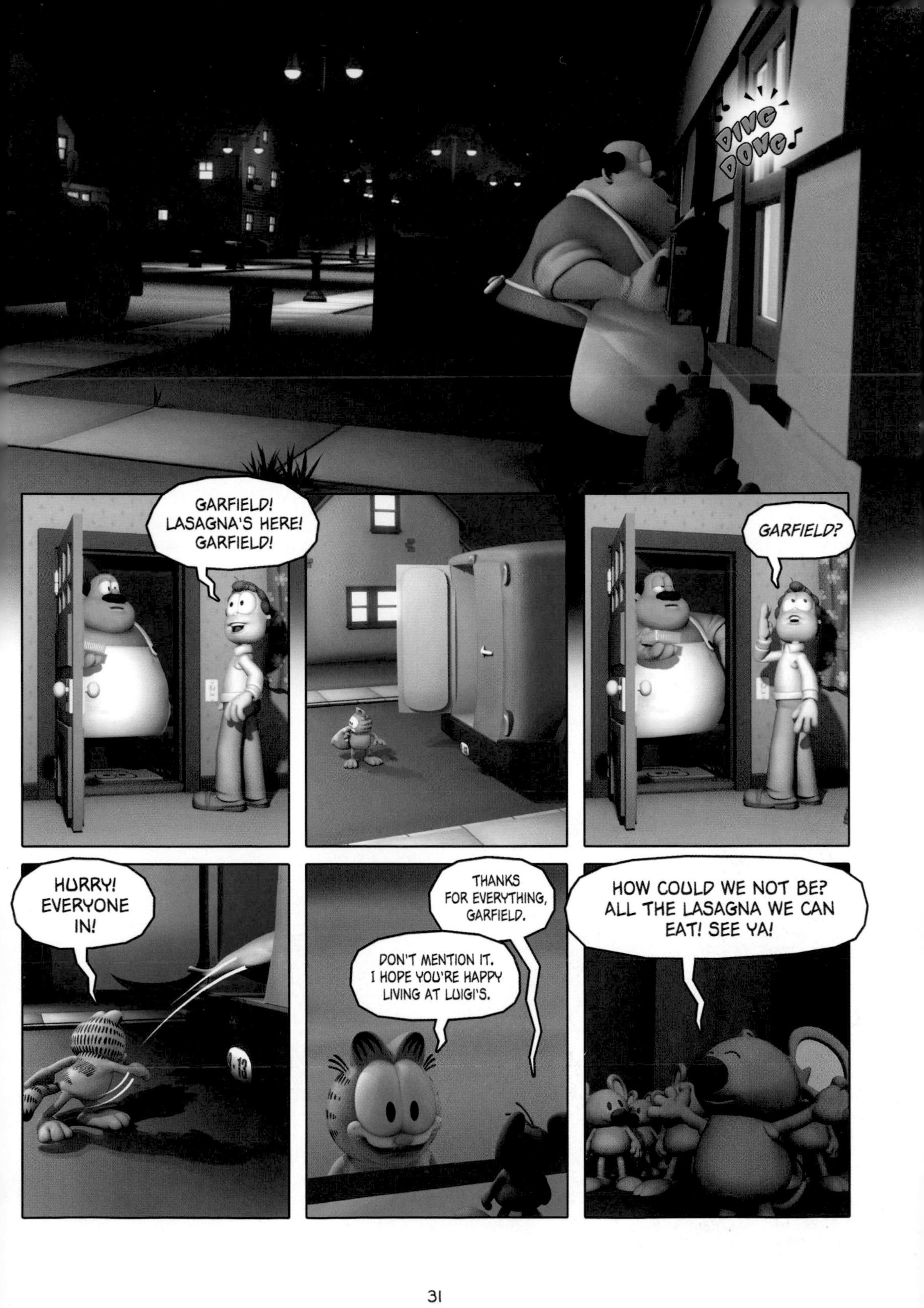
DING DONG
GARFIELD! LASAGNA'S HERE! GARFIELD!
GARFIELD?
HURRY! EVERYONE IN!
THANKS FOR EVERYTHING, GARFIELD.
DON'T MENTION IT. I HOPE YOU'RE HAPPY LIVING AT LUIGI'S.
HOW COULD WE NOT BE? ALL THE LASAGNA WE CAN EAT! SEE YA!

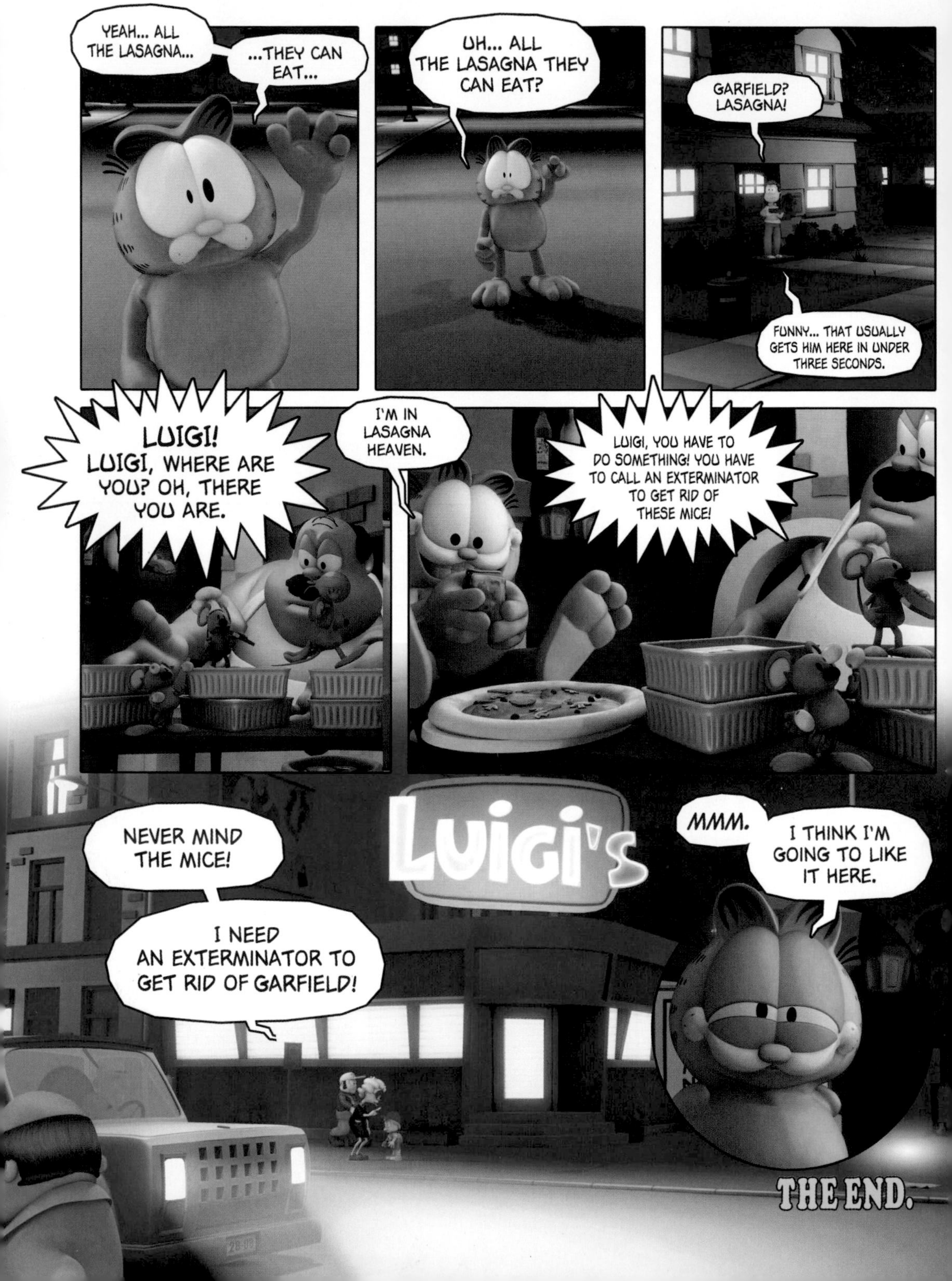

YEAH... ALL THE LASAGNA...
...THEY CAN EAT...
UH... ALL THE LASAGNA THEY CAN EAT?
GARFIELD? LASAGNA!
FUNNY... THAT USUALLY GETS HIM HERE IN UNDER THREE SECONDS.
LUIGI! LUIGI, WHERE ARE YOU? OH, THERE YOU ARE.
I'M IN LASAGNA HEAVEN.
LUIGI, YOU HAVE TO DO SOMETHING! YOU HAVE TO CALL AN EXTERMINATOR TO GET RID OF THESE MICE!
Luigi's
NEVER MIND THE MICE!
I NEED AN EXTERMINATOR TO GET RID OF GARFIELD!
MMM.
I THINK I'M GOING TO LIKE IT HERE.
THE END.

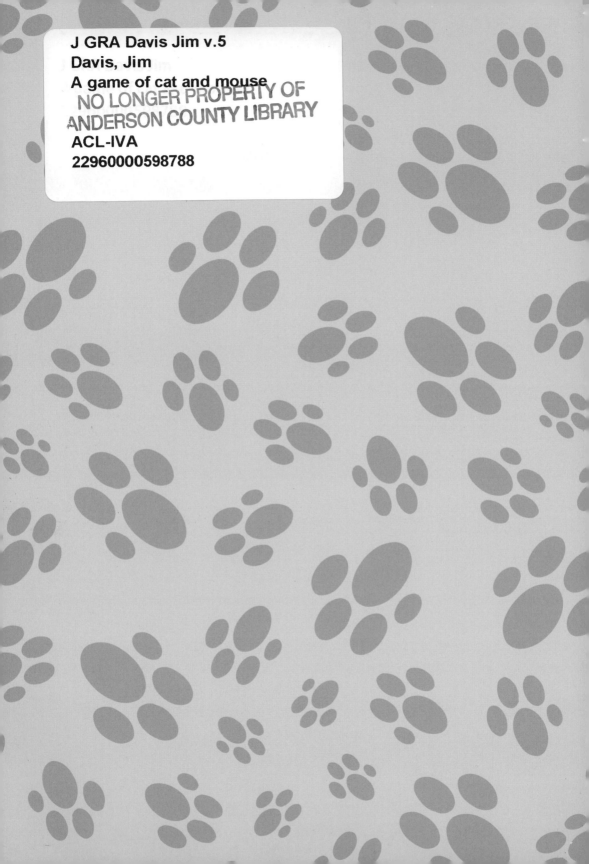